I0587135

COMMANDING THE TIDES

LORDS OF THE ABYSS

MICHELLE M. PILLOW

MICHELLE M. PILLOW® - MICHELLEPILLOW.COM

ABOUT COMMANDING THE TIDES

PARANORMAL UNDERWATER
SHAPESHIFTER ROMANCE

Merman Iason doesn't understand why the woman he's trying to rescue seems insistent he save anyone but her. Duty bound to save whoever he can, he takes her to Atlantes, his home beneath the waves. But a watery grave isn't the only thing threatening his new charge's life. To try and save her from a mortal illness would mean possible disgrace and being banned from ever swimming in the ocean again. But what else can he do? From the first moment he saw her, she had command over his heart.

Dragon Lords Series
Barbarian Prince
Perfect Prince
Dark Prince
Warrior Prince
His Highness The Duke
The Stubborn Lord
The Reluctant Lord
The Impatient Lord
The Dragon's Queen

Lords of the Var® **Series**
The Savage King

The Playful Prince
The Bound Prince
The Rogue Prince
The Pirate Prince

Captured by a Dragon-Shifter Series
Determined Prince
Rebellious Prince
Stranded with the Cajun
Hunted by the Dragon
Mischievous Prince
Headstrong Prince

Space Lords Series
His Frost Maiden
His Fire Maiden
His Metal Maiden
His Earth Maiden
His Woodland Maiden

Dynasty Lords Series

Seduction of the Phoenix

Temptation of the Butterfly

To learn more about the Qurilixen World series of books and to stay up to date on the latest book list visit www.MichellePillow.com

AUTHOR UPDATES

To stay informed about when a new book in the series installments is released, sign up for updates:

michellepillow.com/author-updates

To Jessica, Kitten and Chell, thank you for all your help! To all my wonderful readers, your continued support means the universe to me.

CHAPTER 1

IASON THE HUNTER swam through the murky waters of the dark ocean. The sound of drowning victims echoed in his head. No matter how often he heard such despair, it never became easier. He wished he could save them, but all he could do was push the humans toward the surface and wish them luck. Besides, by the time he and his fellow hunters arrived at the human ship, the hull was sinking down into the ocean's depths. It had been too late for many of the mortals and there was no land for miles.

Though, honestly, perhaps saving them was crueler than letting them drown. They were in the middle of the ocean, no sign of rescue vibrating in the water. Chances were their bodies would weaken and

MICHELLE M. PILLOW

they would die a long, horrible death. If they managed to float on a raft, the hot sun and lack of drinking water would kill them. But, what else could he do? Wasn't a small chance better than none?

Seeing a flash of silvery black fins in the water, Iason frowned. That was not the creature they hunted. He watched carefully, seeing the subtle flash again.

'*I think I see Brutus or Demon,*' Iason said to his fellow hunters, using their mind link. All the Merr could communicate by telepathy in the water.

Caderyn, to his right, looked at him in surprise. '*Where?*'

Iason pointed down toward the ocean's floor.

Iason was part of a team of three Merr hunters—himself, Caderyn and Solon—known simply as the *Hunters*. There were twelve Merr hunters in total, split up into four teams of three. Three brothers, Rigel, Demon and Brutus were another team, the *Warriors*. Rigel, the youngest and smallest of the three, led the team. There were also the *Knights* led by Cain and the *Soldiers* led by Hrafn. Both the Knights and Soldiers were taking a much needed break from hunting while the other two teams took up their duties.

Solon was the leader of the Hunters because he

chose to carry the vial around his neck. It was filled with a liquid that would paralyze the scylla so they could catch it. The liquid was the only way to stop a scylla. Unfortunately, if spilled, it could paralyze the Merr as well. Carrying it was a job that took much concentration. Solon had final say when it came to capturing the creature because it was he who needed to get into position.

The three Hunters had worked together for years and none of them had black tails. Caderyn's was purple. Iason's was green. Solon's was green-gold.

Iason motioned his hand. In the distance they saw Brutus emerge to push a drowning human toward the surface. The mortal man was still alive and grabbed a floating piece of the ship's debris. Brutus swam quickly under his legs, making a current that would drift the survivor away from the shipwreck.

'*Rigel must be close,*' Caderyn said. His dark brown hair drifted around his head, floating briefly before his stark purple eyes. The silver purple of his tail whipped once, pushing him up higher. Like all Merr, Caderyn's tail and fins matched the color of his eyes. '*What are they doing here? Were they sent to aid us?*'

'*They track a scylla, same as us.*' Solon joined

them, gliding his arms back and forth to hover in the water. His hazel eyes glowed slightly as he looked around, trying to track their prey. The vial around his neck drifted easily with his movements. *'Rigel says it's been evading them. I told him we have the same problem.'*

'That means there are two old ones in the water this night.' Iason frowned.

The scylla were dangerous creatures. They were spirits of the water, mindless, reckless, forever searching. Two scylla together would be strong enough to push any one of them out of the water. One of the only things that could kill the Merr was surface air. It would burn the skin, but if breathed, it would destroy.

'Aye,' Solon answered.

Caderyn swam toward Brutus, his long tail waving in the water to propel him forward. Iason could hear him calling out. Brutus turned in surprise. Soon, all six Merr were gathered together.

Brutus and his twin brother, Demon, were two of the largest of the Merr race. They were identical in every aspect, from their long black hair to their matching dark eyes. Even their fins were the same silvery black color. It made them nearly invisible in the deep waters, even to their own kind sometimes. Their younger brother, Rigel, was a lighter version of the twins. His hair was dark, but not black, and his eyes were gray. When the sunlight shone through the waves in a certain way, his silver fins looked like ship's metal floating in the water.

'You've been away from Ataran longer,' Iason said to the other team. 'We will help you catch yours and then go for ours. You need to get home before you lose your way.'

The Warriors nodded. All knew they could only stay away from Ataran soil for two weeks before going mad. Once madness set in, they would never find their way back alone. Even going past a week was pushing it.

'He's a big one,' Brutus warned.

'Slipped by us twice already,' Demon added. 'Tore up this ship, though I see now that he had help. We were wondering why it went down so fast for as big as it was.'

A cold rush of current, colder than usual, crept over them. They turned to the man Brutus had helped to save. The human's legs kicked violently, and they saw the shadowed form of a scylla beneath him.

'*By All the Gods!*' Solon swore. '*It is huge.*'

All six mermen swarmed into action. Rigel tore the vial from his neck, ready to blow. The creature began to drift, nothing more than a dark spot in the water. It was a near shapeless, faceless shadowing. It made a dash past Brutus and Demon. The two brothers cut it off. Iason and Solon crowded its sides as Caderyn swam below. Rigel blew the vial. The creature bucked up, knocking the human up, tossing him high above the surface. Iason heard the man scream but ignored it.

Both Brutus and Demon latched onto the scylla, fighting it as they dragged it deep into the ocean. The creature soon became subdued and the hunters were able to drag it more easily.

Rigel waved at Iason. '*Go. Find the second. I'll push this mortal up and will follow my team.*'

Iason looked at Caderyn. His friend closed his eyes, sensing the water. Suddenly, he pointed into the distance. '*That way.*'

'*What is that noise?*' Solon asked.

'*Another boat?*' Iason frowned. He reached out his hands, feeling the small vibrations of the water.

'*Not another one,*' Caderyn growled in frustration. '*What are they all doing out this far in the ocean?*

Why tonight? This should have been an open water hunt.'

'*Come on, let's bag it and drag it before it takes this ship down as well. I'm ready to go home.'* Iason waved his hand and pointed to where he detected the ship. His companions nodded in agreement. Swimming as fast as he could, he pushed into the distance.

CHAPTER 2

CASSANDRA NEVIN SAW her life flash before her eyes as the freezing water surrounded her. She'd had a bad feeling about this trip, but then she had a bad feeling about everything since the doctor told her she was dying of cancer. Bone cancer. Not much to be done for it, not as late as they had caught it. She'd refused treatment, refused to prolong her life only to live in a bed withering away. Already, she'd outlived her initial prognosis, perhaps by sheer will, perhaps by dumb luck. Waiting for death to come for her had become her own sad little game, and she honestly knew that, when it did, she wouldn't be surprised. Her parents didn't understand, or maybe they did, but they didn't agree with her choice.

No one on the ship knew except Ned Devenpeck. He was the head of the scientific expedition she was on. Cassandra was sure he just felt sorry for her and that was why he let her tag along with only a few classes of college science under her belt. She wasn't one for charity, but in this instance she had taken it and gladly.

She knew that the other scientists were irritated with her because she didn't know what she was doing. Cassandra didn't care. Why should she? Life was too short to care about anything. It's why she left school before graduating with a degree. Everyone she knew cried when they saw her, even her parents. She preferred the angry scientists to the constant pity, preferred to be yelled at and hated than to be treated like a dog on its last legs.

As the boat sank, hit from below by some creature the scientists couldn't name, she'd been scared—scared of dying alone at sea, scared of that final icy breath of water, scared of the unknown beneath her in the darkness.

"Aliens?" someone had suggested as the boat was nearly tipped over on its side.

"New species of Deep Ocean fish rising to the surface to feed?" another scientist had proposed.

They were all great minds, rational minds, but the truth was, they didn't know any more than she did, about what had attacked the ship. The scientists had tried to catch the animal in a net. They had some success, but the creature had freed itself before they could pull it up.

Cassandra had managed to get a small peek of their attacker in the water. If she had to guess, she would say the creature looked like a merman. But who would believe such a wild story from the woman who didn't even know the exact procedure to draw basic surface samples? So, she'd kept the observation to herself. It was quite possible that the pain meds were starting to affect her mind anyway. Since it was nighttime, she'd already taken her dose so she could sleep through the night.

So, yes, she'd been scared of dying the instant the water took her body. But now, as she stopped struggling and let the black ocean have her, a strange acceptance came over her. She was dying. What more picturesque means than at sea? Her body drifting forever in the ocean, parts of her traveling, in time, to every port? It was poetic, in a beautifully sad way.

The inky water surrounded her, blackened by

the night sky. She watched the spotlight from the boat glancing over her head as she was pulled down and saw the faint outlines of scientists fighting for life. Cassandra felt bad for them and had to look away. The cold stung, but it was better to feel than to not. Soon numbness would set in and it wouldn't hurt anymore. The cold was nothing compared to the deep ache in her bones, the constant agony, the lethargy of pain pills.

A glimmer came from in front of her, a green shimmering light unlike anything she would have expected in the dark Abyss. Hands reached for her, human hands. At first, she waited for them to touch her, but then they did and she struggled as they grasped onto her arms. They were real, too real to be a hallucination.

No! I'm ready. Let me go! she thought. She struggled against the hands, fighting them. *Let me go! Save someone else. I don't want to wither away. I want to drift.*

'*Let me help you,*' a strange voice ordered in her head. The speaker was male, a voice she didn't know.

Was it a being from the afterlife come to fetch her? An angel?

'*Stop struggling, woman. I won't hurt you,*' he ordered. The man who tried to hold on to her was no angel. She had little time to think about the impossibility of her hearing him in her head.

Cassandra opened her mouth wide, ready to take the water into her lungs, ready for it to be over. Let him save someone else, someone with a chance. Instead of the salty brine, warm lips pressed to hers. In her shock, she stopped struggling. No one had kissed her since she was diagnosed. Her boyfriend had left her. Oh, he'd tried to stick around, but he'd been too creeped out by it all and soon found the tiny excuse he needed to bail.

She wrapped her arms around the man's neck, slipping her tongue past his lips. He tasted sweet, like fruit wine. Her body was starved of contact, for a feeling beyond that of sterile examination gloves and clinical exams. It has been a long time since someone just held her.

Her would-be rescuer jerked as she kissed him. Why wouldn't he be surprised? She was dying in his arms, selfishly taking one last moment for herself.

The man tried to swim with her body. Cassandra didn't care. She let him pull her. Her lungs were burning and soon it would be too late for her. It felt good to be held, even as the darkness threatened. She clung to the warmth. Death was close and she welcomed it, thankful that she wasn't going to be alone when it finally came for her.

Her lungs were on fire with the need for air. A hand thrust into her hair. The mouth against hers widened, his lips slipping over hers. Then, as blackness consumed her, she smiled. She would never have to feel another thing again. The pain was over.

CHAPTER 3

'Damn humans!' Iason swore. If they wouldn't have interfered, wouldn't have tried to capture Caderyn in a net, the hunters would have stopped the scylla in time. The scylla was the humans' true enemy out here on the water, not the Merr. But, because of the mortals' interference, there were now two ships lost at sea this night.

'*Let me help you,*' he said angrily to himself as he tried to save the woman's life. They had captured their prey but not before it crashed into the second ship, sending the onboard passengers to their deaths. He attempted to latch his mouth onto the drowning woman's to help her breathe beneath the waves. '*Stop struggling, woman. I won't hurt you.*'

Iason almost let go of the woman in his arms as

she kneed him in the gut, or at least he told himself to let her go. Had he been in human form, she would have kicked him in the balls. With a tail, it didn't hurt as badly, but it still smarted. Who was he to save someone who didn't want to be rescued?

Iason gripped her tighter. He was about to knock her unconscious with a head butt to the temple when she surprised him by kissing him, really kissing him. And not just the breathing kiss he'd been trying to give her, but an intimate kiss—the type of kiss a woman gives a man when she desires him. He felt her tongue mingling with the chilly saltwater that surrounded them. There was no hesitation, only the desperate, pleading kiss of a woman starved. It had been so long, so many centuries since he'd been kissed by a woman that for a moment he was too stunned to move.

Not that he kissed men. He didn't kiss anyone. Unless the pleasure nymph counted, and that piece of machinery had no use for his mouth.

And why exactly was he thinking of such things right now? In the middle of the dark ocean, far from home?

Desire stirred within him, hot and potent. He couldn't help his response as he returned the soft embrace, pulling the woman's thin body closer. But, as her mouth quit moving so violently against his, he was shaken back to reality. She was dying. The woman had stopped struggling, and he was finally able to seal his lips around hers.

His gills fluttered as he forced breath down her lungs, filtering the sea water for her so she could breathe. It wasn't long before she stopped moving altogether, passing out, and he was glad for it. It was hard enough breathing for two, without the person trying to beat him while he did it, or trying to kiss him for that matter.

Iason flicked his tail, swimming backwards as he dragged the frail human down into the black Abyss. She was skinny, almost nothing but skin and bones. Chances were she wouldn't survive the dive down anyway, but Merr law said he had to try. A small chance was better than none.

'*Got one,*' Iason said to his fellow hunters, not breaking his lips from the woman's, as he watched Solon drag the scylla ahead of him. For all intents and purposes the hunt had been a success. Two scylla were captured this night and would roam the ocean no more. But, he couldn't help feeling bad for those lives lost at sea.

'*I don't envy you the trouble,*' Solon answered. '*I'd much rather have my burden than yours, friend.*'

Iason pulled the woman closer, adjusting her in his arms. She was as cold as the ocean and the heat from his body would only sustain her for so long. She didn't move, didn't fight, but he could detect her heart beating lightly against the sensitive skin of his chest. He didn't hold out much hope. Not many humans made the dive down and this one had a poor start.

Their laws were clear. Women were rare in their world and if one was condemned to a watery death and could be saved, they were to save them. Humans were so fragile that often they didn't survive the dive down into Deep Ocean, especially after the trauma of a shipwreck. Many times, the hunters tried to save them, only to have them die on the way down. That's why they only ever chanced it with those already fated to perish at sea.

Swimming into the depths of the Abyss, Iason left the wreckage behind him. It was dark, but his Merr eyes pierced the black waters with ease. His gaze gave off a softened glow as he scanned his surroundings. Sensing the creatures of the deep ocean as if they were part of himself, he felt them moving, swimming, hunting. For the most part, they avoided the Merr hunters altogether.

Iason concentrated on breathing as he pulled the

woman closer. Why did she have to kiss him like that? Now, not only did he have to fight to breathe for two, he had to try and ignore the taste of her on his mouth as he breathed. It was pure torture, but he couldn't break the seal. To do so at this depth would mean her death. The pressure of the Abyss would kill her just as surely as the water in her lungs.

Iason felt every slender curve of her body against his. Her breasts were soft, making a hot wave of desire flood his veins. It had been a very long time, centuries to be exact, since any of the hunters had mated with something other than a pleasure nymph. None of them had wives to go home to.

The further away he got from the wreckage, the more ocean life swam around him, becoming fiercer in appearance. They looked nothing like their surface dwelling counterparts. Gliding downward, he weaved, automatically dodging a baby squid. It was twice as long as he was. The deep sea creatures didn't bother him, and Iason ignored them in turn.

He swam faster, letting the water glide past them as he headed straight down into the Abyss. Trying to will her to take the heat from his body, he felt her tremble. He didn't have long before she was dead.

CHAPTER 4

IASON DRIFTED into the cave leading to Ataran. He had made it, and, somehow, the woman hadn't died on the way down. She still could, but for the moment, she was alive. Her heart beat faintly against him, but it did beat.

It was with a surreal sense of pleasure that he broke the surface. Pulling his lips from hers, he gasped for breath. The air was sweet with the smell of sea flowers. The woman coughed, but otherwise breathed the cave air just fine.

"She lives?" Solon asked, his tail already transformed back into legs. They were in Crystal Caves, in the sacred heart of their city. In their human forms they didn't use telepathy. They could, if they wanted to open themselves up to it, they just didn't. Too many voices ringing in their heads tended to make them edgy. Usually only spouses communicated with the mind on land. For those who were married, a private connection came easily.

'Aye,' Iason directed with his mind, unable to use words until he was transformed back into his human form. He pushed the woman up onto the narrow rocky ledge along the cave's surface. It was shallow enough that the water didn't cover her face. 'She lives.'

"I'll take the scylla to the holding cells," Solon said, lifting his barely visible burden off the ground. "Then I'm going to rest. Good luck with that one."

Iason nodded, chuckling to himself. He flipped his fin, pushing up from the water to sit by the woman. Twisting around, he brought his tail from the ocean and brushed the water off with his fingers. They dried quickly, and he watched as flesh replaced his tail. When he could again stand as a man, he lifted the woman from the ledge and pulled her onto dry land.

Laying her on the ground, he breathed heavily from the ordeal of hunting and rescuing. He knelt beside her, taking the opportunity to study her face. Before, he hadn't gotten a good look at her in the dark water as he tried to subdue her long enough to latch his mouth to hers. She was a tiny thing with dark red hair that fanned over her pale features. He detected a sprinkling of freckles across her nose. They were adorable.

Now that she was safe, he felt the soft press of her lips as if they were still kissing him. The breathing kiss was more intimate than other kisses practiced during love making, because it transferred the gift of life, but the feel of her tongue invading the depths of his mouth was by far the more arousing.

Her clothes were strange. She wore thin, stretchy material over her legs. Even wet it was soft to the touch. A thick black stripe lined the sides from hip to ankle. A human soldier uniform? He'd seen scavenged books that had drawings of such striped markings on the legs. The woman hardly appeared to have the body of a trained fighter. She was too delicate for that.

Over her thin form, she wore a tight black top. It formed to every detail of her figure. Iason stared at the hard peaks of her nipples and mindlessly reached out to touch one. How long had it been since he'd touched a woman's flesh, felt its softness molding against his harder frame? He tried, but he couldn't remember the exact texture of soft flesh pressed to his naked human form. He imagined it would be much like the pleasure nymph. His finger brushed her breast, and he jerked his hand back, realizing what he was doing. Swallowing, he regained control over his suddenly lurid thoughts. Over the tight black top, she wore a soft jacket that matched the pants. He tugged the sides of it, dropping it over her breasts to hide the tempting nipples from view.

Hearing a splash behind him, he knew Caderyn had made it back. By the time he turned around, his fellow hunter was already out of the water and brushing the droplets from his tail, which transformed into legs. Iason watched in surprise as Caderyn lifted a dark haired woman from the water. Two women were saved this night? Caderyn brought his woman to lie beside Iason's.

Iason stood and the two hunters stared down at the mortal women. The dark haired one was just as pale as his, but her features were more filled out. He wondered why he would be so attracted to one and not the other. Perhaps it was because it was her life he had saved. Or perhaps it had been the desperation of her kiss when he saved her.

Iason swallowed. His blood was stirred with desire. It was bad enough that after the hunt he always needed to seek sexual release, for passions ran deep within his kind, but to have that need aroused by a flesh and blood woman? It was torture. The pleasure of release eased Merr tensions and centered their thoughts. If they refused to cure themselves of the 'affliction', they could get sick.

"You know what this means," Caderyn said, still staring down at the unconscious woman with black hair.

"Aye," Iason answered, studying the red head, wondering what he should do with her now that he had her here. He tried to remember what humans needed, but it had been so long.

"Do you think you'll keep this one?"

"Let us see her temperament when she wakes," Iason said, remembering how she fought him in the water. The flaming color of her hair didn't bode well either. It was said that redheads were harder to control and a faint, long forgotten memory tugging at the back of his mind told him it was true.

Iason knew that he'd done what he could and didn't feel bad for taking the woman from her world to his. The gods would decide whether or not these women lived. All the hunters could do was try to save them. She'd made the dive down, that was a start. But why wasn't she waking up? Would they save them only to lose them?

"Aye," Caderyn agreed.

Both men sighed.

"Now what?" Iason glanced at his friend and scratched the back of his head. "Do you remember what to do with them once we save them? It's been many years since we got one this far."

"We should take them to Althea," Caderyn leaned over, sighing as if he'd come to a great decision. Not bothering to find clothes, he lifted the dark haired woman off the ground, cradling her before his chest. Iason nodded and did the same. "The healer will know what to do with them."

They were in the palace of the Atlas, capital city of Ataran. The cave walls were covered in sparkling precious gems, which was the reason they called them the Crystal Caves. The colorful stones reflected torches, vibrantly lighting the way. Iason carried the woman to the entrance of the cave. Two guards stared at them and then at the women in awe.

Both guards wore the traditional Ionic *chiton* of the Merr people. The short, white shirt was a rectangular piece of material folded in half and sewn up the side. It pinned along the sleeves and fell just over the knees, leaving the calves bear. A single stranded belt cinched the material about the waist. The *chalmys* cloak draped over one shoulder in a broad sweep of green. It was pinned at the shoulder with a circular gold brooch, engraved with the ancient Merr symbol of the sun. Like most Merr, the guards wore strapped leather sandals on their feet.

"I saw you bagged the scylla, my lords," Vitus, a darker complexioned guard said, nodding in approval. "Well done."

"Are these women alive?" asked Brennus, a tall blond who hoped to someday be a hunter. His interest in them was evident by the glint in his eyes. The only way that would happen was if King Lucius appointed more teams or if one of the team members were killed. The only way they would be killed is if they didn't make it back to Ataran on time and were lost forever at sea, or if they were dragged to the surface world and forced to breath the mortal air.

"Aye," Caderyn agreed.

Iason adjusted the frail woman in his arms, wishing he knew what to call her. Her lips parted in breath, and it was hard not to brush his mouth to hers. He ignored the guards, unable to speak as he stared at her mouth, remembering her kiss.

What had prompted her to kiss him in that moment? The woman had been dying. She should have tried to reach the surface, not kiss him. The woman shivered in his arms, and he hugged her wet body closer.

When Iason didn't speak, Caderyn answered the guards, "We take them to Althea. Inform King Lucius. Also, call the scavengers. Two ships went down. Solon will give you directions."

"Aye," Brennus agreed, though he didn't run off right away, as he helped Vitus to push a large round stone before the cave opening to block it off. The men gave one last longing glance toward the women.

The city architects had glazed the bricks of the wall with a mixture made from the gemstones, which gave them an almost glowing blue cast. Light was reflected from outside during the day, but at night torches were lit throughout the palace halls.

The blue glazed stone of the palace was accented with decorative yellow and white tiles. The tiles formed beautifully intricate patterns. The halls were clean and uncluttered. Large arches passed overhead as they walked out of the cave room to the main palace hall. Caderyn nodded at the few people he passed, receiving several curious stares in return. Iason tried to do the same, but he was mesmerized by the redhead's mouth. Her lips were so full, so bowed.

Why did she kiss him?

Why like that?

Althea the Healer lived within the palace walls so it didn't take long to reach her home. Without asking permission to enter, Caderyn pushed aside the beaded door and stepped in, calling, "Lady Althea. We have need of your assistance."

The home was like many in the palace, a large square living area, an office, adjoining sleeping and bathing rooms. Those in the palace took their meals together in the hall so there was no need for a kitchen or place to dine. In the living area there were paintings on the walls and minimal furniture. The low bench-like couches had no backs. Their wool-covered seats were intricately woven and quite beautiful. They should be with all the years the craftsmen had to perfect their skills. The floors were bare and swept clean.

Althea came from her office, taking one look at the men, with their damp hair and naked bodies, before glancing briefly over the unconscious mortals. She nodded for them to follow her. In her office, on the far side of the room, there were two low beds. A small stone desk stood in the corner and rolled scrolls were placed along the wall in diamond shaped cubbies. The men laid the women on the beds and stood.

The healer was a slender woman, draped in the finest linen material. Oil was rubbed into the weave, making the dress shine. The light green material was plain, woven with a darker green along the edges in the pattern of seaweed. Two pins held the garment at the shoulders, leaving the arms bare. Her brown hair was pulled back from her face, fastened in an intricate coil around the crown.

"Help me to remove their clothing," Althea ordered. "Mortals cannot be left wet."

Iason readily agreed, almost desperate in his high state of arousal to see more of the woman than her pretty lips. His body was hot for her, from touching and holding her. He slipped the jacket off her shoulders and pulled the pants from her hips before ripping through the tight top, jerking the thin material apart. Out of the corner of his eye, he saw Caderyn cut his woman's clothes off more delicately with shears. Iason didn't care if he looked like a brute. Althea told him to shed her clothing, and he was shedding her clothing the fastest way he knew how.

Leaning back, he admired his handiwork. His gut tightened and a frown marred his brow. Compared to the toned figure of Caderyn's woman, his was too slender. Perhaps this woman was a slave. Her bones jutted out near her hips. She was so thin, practically starved until there was no meat on her bones. Iason wasn't repulsed. If anything, he felt all the more protective of her.

Her breasts were small, the nipples pink little dots on her pale flesh. He wanted to touch them, to touch her. A thatch of curly red hair graced the apex of her thighs. It called to him. He wanted to stroke it, to smell her flesh. His heart leaped in his chest. The way she was laying caused her thighs to fall open. It had been so long since he smelled the unique fragrance from a woman's nether region. His cock stirred, growing painfully aroused, more so than it had already been.

Iason started to reach for her, eager to heal her on his own, but forced himself to hold back. For him to heal her would not be right. Men only healed their wives. Otherwise, the healer was called.

In Ataran they never knew bodily sickness. The only injuries most of the Merr people sustained were accidental or on the practice field, though they did not battle anymore except in the games. Or, for the few chosen to be hunters, they could be injured on the hunt. Only the hunters ventured so close to the dangerous mortal surface.

"One wound I can tend, my lords, the other...." Althea laughed.

Iason glanced at Althea. She was smiling as she

nodded at his friend's leg. Blood trailed from the wound Caderyn had received while captured in the human's net. But that wasn't what Althea teased them about. They'd both become fully erect from staring at the women.

"Here, put these on," Althea tossed them two plain garments she kept for just such an occasion. Iason draped the material around his body, knotting it at the shoulder. "Dress your own wound Caderyn and you both should tend to the other affliction. Come back in an hour and I will tell you what I've discovered."

Both men nodded, leaving the mortals to the healer. Iason looked back at Caderyn, ready to speak, but the man stood in the doorway staring at the women. Iason cleared his throat to get his friend's attention. Caderyn gave him a sheepish grin and followed him out of the healer's home.

CHAPTER 5

"Two of them," Iason mused to Caderyn, walking down the hall toward the hunters' wing in the palace. "What are the odds? Do you think they'll live this time?"

"The humans or the scylla?" Caderyn asked softly, stretching his arms over his head. The halls were quiet and they were free to talk without being overheard.

"Both I suppose," Iason said. "It would be a shame to lose any of them."

"You know as well as I that the odds are slim," Caderyn said. "I'm surprised we even got them this far."

Iason laughed softly. "The women or the scylla?"

"The women," Caderyn said, grinning. Boasting

somewhat, though rightly so, he added, "I knew we would get the scylla. We are the Hunters. We always bag our prey."

"Aye," Iason nodded. They had a right to be proud. All hunters worked long and hard, and they also took many risks—risks other Merr were unable or unwilling to take. They turned into the hunters' wing of the palace. Doors lined the sides forming a row down one wall. Iason reached for the first door. "I will meet you in an hour."

"Aye," Caderyn answered. Neither man spoke for a moment, but they both knew what the other was thinking. They were worried the women might not survive. "I will see you in an hour."

Iason shut the door quietly behind him. With a tug, he wearily unknotted the cloak, letting it fall on the floor as he walked. His body was sore. The scylla had slammed him into the hull of the boat. Stretching, he glanced down his form. His back wasn't nearly as sore as the affliction between his legs. His cock was so hard he could probably smash rocks with it.

Iason went to his sleeping room first. Grabbing a key off the top of a narrow wardrobe, he unlocked it. The wardrobes were standard issue for hunters—the best pleasure instruments the Merr inventors could come up with. Inside was everything he needed to pleasure himself.

The centerpiece of his collection was the pleasure nymph. Designed to look like a real woman, her body was soft and almost lifelike. If he were to turn her on, she would move her body against his. She blinked. She breathed. She sighed. The only things she didn't do were think or speak. Her head was bald, her eyes closed. They would remain so until he put the discs hanging on the inside of the wardrobe door into her to program his desired colorings.

Iason absently touched the nymph's breast. His cock throbbed. The Merr called their unreleased sexual desires the affliction because they were convinced that it was a further punishment from the gods that they would be so sexually driven and not have any vessel in which to release themselves. That was why the women they had saved were considered a blessing and a great responsibility. For, through them, hopefully someone on their world would find not only a lover, but a mate to spend this eternity with. Friends were great, but there was something to be envied in the soft looks couples shared. Iason would take their greatest quarrels just for an ounce of their happiness.

The pleasure nymph was a sad replacement for a

real woman, but what else were the Merr to do? He thought of the redhead's flesh beneath his hands as he'd stripped her. With the image so fresh in his mind, he found the nymph lacking.

Unmated Merr women, of which there were very few, were the same way. They were given pleasure instruments to deal with their afflictions. Taking a lover from amongst the population was discouraged. Eternity was too long a time to hold a grudge over relationships that ended badly. Some Merr were still bearing the impact of such relationships—like King Lucius and his exiled lover, Maia.

Maia wanted to be queen. When Lucius refused, she grew so enraged that several believed she actually went mad, taking several women with her into the forest. They called themselves the Olympians and opposed everything the Merr stood for. They were a bitter, angry group of women that the rest of the Merr tried to avoid. For the most part it wasn't hard. They tended to keep to themselves, hidden beyond the city in the forest. Though, it was said they kept captured men prisoners to indulge their pleasure. There were times when the loneliness got to be too much and he thought about taking a walk in the Olympian's woods so that they could take him prisoner.

Iason pulled his hand from the nymph's breast and instead opened a jar of white herbal cream. Dipping his hand inside, he instantly felt the tingle of it working on his fingers. He closed the lid and put the jar away, careful to lock the wardrobe. It was rare, but pleasure instruments had been stolen before. It was suspected they were traded to the Olympians, but the Merr had no solid proof of who took them.

Lying on his back, Iason closed his eyes. He remembered the redhead's mouth on his, kissing him with such eagerness and desperation, salty from the ocean water and yet fresh at the same time with her own taste. Slathering his cock, he rubbed the thick white cream over his stiff length, making sure he also coated his balls and the sensitive flesh hidden underneath. It felt good, almost hot, as it tingled on his skin. He rubbed it on his nipples, letting it tingle there too.

Stroking himself, he enjoyed the glide of his hand on his body. He pinched the tip, squeezed the shaft, and pumped his fist over his cock from root to end. Bending his knees, his body really got into it. He thrust his hips up off the bed, pushing with his heels. His balls ached for attention and he cupped them, rolling them in his palm.

Her kiss, her soft mouth, her tongue...

MICHELLE M. PILLOW

It was easy to imagine the redhead above him, taking him all in. He refused to think of her overly thin frame as he concentrated on the memory of her bowed lips. He wondered if her pussy would be tight on him, as he fisted himself harder. Oh, yeah, just like that—tight and wet, so wet the cream of her body would drip down all over his thighs and stomach.

Iason tried to hold back, fighting release as he enjoyed his fantasy. He flipped over, sliding a soft pillow beneath his chest. Pushing up, he kept his fist formed in a circle as he pumped his hips against it. His butt tensed with each thrust.

"Argh," he grunted softly, unable to help the sound. He bit his lip, so close to spilling his seed.

Iason pictured the woman's parted thighs, the thatch of her red hair. He wanted his fist to be her so badly that it made his chest ache. She had to live. He had to possess her body—tradition be damned. He would make her choose him.

He pumped faster, grunting louder as his fantasy took hold. The redheaded woman was his, all his. He wouldn't give her the choice of another mate. If any of the Merr asked him for the right to pursue her, he would refuse them. She was his, all his. If he had to he would take her to his home in the country and lock her away until she chose to be with him, then so be it. That is exactly what he would do.

"Mine," he groaned, pumping faster. "Mine."

Iason would do whatever he had to. He would seduce her, tempt her, woo her, anything short of actual force--for he could never harm her. Whatever it took, whatever laws he had to break, the woman would be his lover. That one kiss had sealed her fate. She would be his, and he would spend the rest of his life making her happy in the decision.

Suddenly, his whole body stiffened. His balls tightened as he arched his back, coming heavily on the bed covers. The release was so good, so much better than he'd remembered having in a long time. He collapsed against the pillow, still holding himself.

It was decided then. The woman would belong to him. Iason sighed, loud and long. The tension drained from his body. Then turning his head to look at the door, he frowned. He didn't even know her name.

"Mine," he whispered.

CHAPTER 6

AFTER SHOWERING IN FRESH WATER, Iason met Caderyn in the hall. An hour had passed quicker than he imagined it would. He'd lost himself in the fantasy of the woman. Iason's stomach was tight with worry over her, but at least the tension of his arousal was gone. He didn't know why exactly, but he had a feeling he was meant to protect her, to help her. Only, with the possessive thoughts rolling through his brain, it was most likely she would need protection from his arduous attentions.

One look at Caderyn's face and he knew the man was just as worried. They silently walked back to the healer's, their steps measured, almost calculatingly so, for when they got to their destination they would discover the fate of the women.

Iason had never been a mean person and was always levelheaded. He could be demanding, sure, but never unfair. Then why did just one little slip of a woman cause his emotions such discord? Why did just the thought of her not choosing him make him so angry he wanted to punch the nearest wall?

He took a deep breath. Perhaps the woman was a sea witch. Maybe her kiss was meant to torture him this way. Even now she could be poisoning his blood.

Never mind that they had never actually run across a living sea witch for nearly a century.

It didn't matter. First she had to live.

She's not dead. I would feel it if she were, he told himself as they paused outside the healer's home. Though he wasn't necessarily sure it was true.

"Healer?" Iason stepped into Althea's home. His voice was a little hoarse. Thinking of the redhead had made his cock stir to half-mast.

A small sense of relief washed over Iason to see the dark haired woman standing in the healer's living room. He looked around for the redhead but didn't see her.

No! His mind screamed. *Not dead. She can't be dead.*

The mortal woman's blue eyes took him in briefly before turning to stare at Caderyn. Iason heard his friend gasp behind him, and it took all his willpower not to laugh. Thinking of the redhead, his amusement faded.

Iason drew the woman's attention back from Caderyn by bowing politely, and said, "Welcome to Ataran, my lady. I am Iason the Hunter."

"Um, Bridget Dutton." Bridget said, her voice hoarse. She wore a long white tunic and looked as if she'd been bathed by Althea after her healing. Appearing almost confused, the woman added, "I'm a scientist with the ESC, Exploratory Science Commission. We were out taking biochemical surface readings off the coast of Florida."

"Welcome, Lady Bridget," Caderyn said from behind him. "I am Caderyn the Hunter."

Iason again glanced around the room, finally staring at the door leading to the office. He waited, hoping to catch a glimpse of the redhead. His throat tightened. It was quiet possible she was dead. He looked at Althea, too scared to go back and see for himself. She couldn't be dead. It had been too long since he'd felt anything like the sensations in his chest, in his body.

"Wait," Bridget said. She looked around again, obviously confused. Iason felt bad for her. Though, truth be told, she seemed to be handling herself quite well. She held up a finger and, without further comment, walked past them. Iason glanced over his shoulder, seeing her leave the room. Caderyn frowned and followed the woman. Since it was Caderyn who had saved her, he was her guardian. He would see to her.

"The other one?" Iason asked when he was alone with the healer.

"Asleep," Althea said. Iason relaxed some. The woman wasn't dead. Then, as the healer continued, he tensed once more. "But she is not well. Until we are sure what is wrong with her, she should be moved from the palace. I doubt she could harm the Merr, but the other mortals..." Althea motioned her hands to the side, help-less. "I don't understand the illness. It is not something I have seen so I cannot say if the sickness will spread or if we can even heal her. There is something inside her blocking my efforts, something deep. We should sepa-rate them for several months, until they are adjusted completely and until we are sure this one will live. If she does not, we must swim her out into the deep ocean far away from here. This is a strange malady she carries."

Hearing Caderyn and Bridget come back in the room, Iason merely nodded at Althea and turned to watch his friend with the woman. Since they had found the women on the same boat, Iason didn't want to upset Lady Bridget in her delicate state by talking about her friend. He wondered just how much she realized about what was happening to her. Bridget would be under a euphoric spell from both Caderyn's and the healer's touches. Hopefully, before the euphoric cloud lifted from her senses, she'd come to accept her new home.

The euphoria happened to all newcomers. It was a way to help them adjust.

Iason glanced at the office doorway. Something about Althea's words struck him as odd. Frowning, he asked, "Others?"

Althea glanced at Bridget. Her voice soft, she said, "Rigel."

Iason slowly nodded. Rigel had brought back a human as well. This hunt just kept getting stranger and stranger. Two scylla in one night and now three human women? It was almost too successful. He shared a look with Caderyn who nodded once. Iason knew that they would talk later.

"Take her, feed her," Althea urged Caderyn. "Let her rest and then take her to Aidan."

"One thing." Iason turned to Bridget. "The other woman. What is her name?"

"Cassandra Nevin," Bridget answered, her voice still hoarse from her bout with the sea.

"Go," Althea urged Caderyn. "Take her."

Caderyn nodded. He motioned for Bridget to follow him. The woman frowned but obeyed. She looked too lost to do anything else.

Iason made a move to go to the back office. Althea held up her hand to stop him. She walked to the door and peeked out into the hall. Satisfied it was empty and they would not be overheard, she turned and came back. Very softly, she said, "You have a choice to make, my lord."

Iason didn't move.

"This woman, Cassandra. There is much illness in her and I cannot extract it all from her system. She's carrying some sort of pain numbing in her blood. I think it is a human medicine. It's keeping me from finding the root of the sickness. Every time I try, I get lightheaded and sick. I've done as much as I dare." Althea again glanced at the door. Her normally composed features looked nervous as she fidgeted with her hands. Turning her eyes down, she hesitated, then whispered, "You are strong, but she will sap your strength if you are around her. It is possible your energy will be enough to heal her body, but at a great cost to you. It will be painful, my lord, very painful for you. Her illness is deep. She was near dead when you found her. I doubt she was even walking around on that ship. I don't think she should have even been alive. Death is in her bones."

Iason stiffened, unsure about how to answer. Althea glanced up at him and then back down. She would not exaggerate and that worried him.

"Do you understand what I'm telling you, my lord? The only way for her to survive is for you to heal her," Althea said, only to stress, *"with all your energies."*

Iason took a deep breath and then another. He understood perfectly. His eyes again strayed to the doorway keeping the woman hidden from view.

"If it comes to it, you must. It is the only way I know of."

"She is not my wife," Iason said, shaking his head in denial. "You speak of breaking the law. If any found out I would never be allowed to hunt again. I would be banned from the ocean, from society. I would be shamed. My honor, my life, everything..."

"Aye, it is true." Althea nodded. She tilted her head to the side, almost pleading. "I tried to cure her, my lord. I haven't the strength for it. Not with two other mortals under my care. There is too much pain. Even if I hadn't healed Lady Bridget, I would not have cured Lady Cassandra. I am too small. You have the strength of the ocean in you. You are a hunter. If anyone can cure her, it is you, my lord, or one of your kind."

Iason nodded. "I cannot ask this of the others. I saved her. She is my responsibility."

Althea rubbed her arms, shivering. "Even now I ache from it. If I knew of a way to make her sleep until it was over, I would."

Iason considered her words. Breaking the law went against his very nature.

"If you will not do this, it is much kinder for us to let her die rather than to make her suffer this agony. No one should have to feel what she does, and once her pain numbing wears off, it will be agony to watch. If that is your decision, the kind thing to do is to put her out of her misery now before she awakens."

"You're sure she'll live if I...?" Iason closed his eyes taking a deep breath. A strange mix of pleasure and pain rolled over him. Just moments earlier he'd sworn to break the law if needs be to possess her, but he never actually thought it would come to that. To give a woman who was not a wife so much healing energy was to most likely bind them forever. It's why it was forbidden. "Will she wake up so we can ask her what she wants? If she chooses, I won't have to..."

"She will not wake from this, not fully. To wish her to do so is too cruel. It is better that she sleeps."

"You're sure this will work? If I...? Then, she will...?"

"Aye," Althea answered, nodding. "Fairly certain, if her will is strong. That is why you must take her to the country so no one will see what you do. Her illness is deep, but it should not spread to any of the others. I only said that earlier to give you the choice. If you decide to heal her, you have my word no one will ever know of it but me."

"Why lie for me?"

"I have my reasons, my lord," Althea said. "First and foremost, I heal. Will you do it? Will you bind her to you?"

"What if she will not have me?" Iason walked toward the office, his stomach tight. Althea didn't respond, not that he expected her to. It wasn't a question she would know the answer to. "We know nothing of each other."

That wasn't exactly true. He knew her taste on his mouth, the feel of her fragile form in his arms. He knew she had needed help and rescuing from more than just a sinking ship. Her thin body could be explained by illness, but perhaps also neglect. Either way, he knew she needed protection.

Iason took a deep breath. It wasn't a big risk, not if he was careful. So long as no one saw him immediately after the healing, he would not get caught. Althea was wise to tell him to go to the country. He would be alone with the woman there. And so long as Cassandra didn't tell anyone later what he'd done to her or about the choice he'd taken away, his reputation and his status as a hunter would be safe.

Seeing Cassandra on the bed, her chest barely moving, her face pale, he swallowed nervously. What kind of person was she? Would she hold this blackmail over his head for an eternity? Would she use it to make unreasonable demands? Make him wait on her hand and foot? Okay, so that last one wouldn't be too bad.

Would she resent him for what he must do to save her? Would she welcome their joining? Would she want him as a lover? As a protector? To his people hunters were prized, but to her? To a human woman who knew nothing of their life? Would she be attracted to him? Or would she banish him from her bed in disgust?

Logic told him to refuse, to let the healer do the best she could for Cassandra. If she died, then fate decided that she would die. Who was he to question the gods' will?

Iason's body burned to possess her, but was that enough? No matter how much her kiss aroused him, lust was not enough to do what Althea asked of him. He would say no to this. It was better, safer for the both of them, if he left Cassandra to the will of the gods.

"My lord?" Althea touched his arm. "You must decide."

Iason closed his eyes briefly. His mouth opened, ready to refuse, but instead he found himself saying, "Aye. I will do it."

He was a fool.

Iason again looked at Cassandra. This decision was insane. He risked everything with it—his station, his honor, his work, his homes and possessions, perhaps even his eternal freedom.

"Go, get ready to leave," Althea said. "Find a cart to put her in. I will explain to the king that you, as her guardian, must take her from here alone. I will not be questioned. With two other mortals here they will not wish to risk the others' health."

Iason nodded once.

"Go, my lord," Althea urged, giving him a light

push. "I will give her all I can so she may make the journey, but you must hurry."

Iason turned from Cassandra, the image of her frail body captured in his mind.

He was such a fool.

CHAPTER 7

"Are you sure you must be the one to take her? There are servants who will gladly go to your home and watch over her for you." Solon glanced to the cart padded with blankets for Cassandra. His hazel-green eyes shone with concern, as a piece of his longer hair whipped into his face. He frowned in irritation, jerking the leather tie from his locks and rebinding the sides back.

"Aye," Iason answered, glancing up from where he stared at the straps of his sandals. The sky was dark blue, abnormally dark for the daytime, yet it was light out. The dome must have shifted with the currents. Inside it, they didn't feel the movements, but the lighting and location of their world did change as they drifted endlessly along the ocean's floor. "I am her guardian. It is my responsibility. If she doesn't make it and I am not there to oversee her care—"

"I understand," Solon broke in. "This way your honor will not be questioned because you handled your responsibility. I cannot order you to stay."

Iason nodded, as he looked around the inner courtyard to the palace. Large arches lifted overhead, leading back inside, back to where Althea prepared Cassandra for the journey. He again questioned the wisdom of his actions, but he would not say the words to Solon. If Solon knew what he risked for a dying mortal, he would be outraged.

He turned to the front gate, seeing a glimpse of their sacred city, Atlas, in the valley below. The palace sat atop a large hill with a long earthen path that led down to the city. Most of the Merr preferred to live outside the city walls in the countryside, but there were a few homes and shops. The roads of Atlas were evenly laid out on a square grid, looking very clean and orderly, except for the center of town which had a circular pattern. Long walls wound all the way around the city. Bright yellow lines ran along the blue glazed stone. Just like inside the palace, it too almost seemed to glow in the light. The images of sea creatures from the Abyss were depicted along the walls, rising off the flat surface. The artistic detail had taken nearly two decades to complete.

"Iason? Iason, are you listening?" Solon asked.

Iason blinked in confusion. He hadn't been listening. "What?"

"Both scylla are alive. We have them chained," Solon said.

Iason nodded. "This was a peculiar hunt, was it not? Two scylla and three mortals. All alive."

"It was a good hunt," Solon said, nodding in satisfaction. "We have done ourselves proud. No doubt the other teams will be sorry they took a break."

"Aye." Iason clasped Solon by the wrist. They squeezed slightly before letting go. "I'm sorry I must leave you. Send word to the country if you have need of me on the hunt. Otherwise, I will stay until she is better."

"I do not wish to claim a woman, but I understand why you must tend to her. Take whatever time you need and do what you must," Solon said. The hunter nodded once before turning to go. Iason watched him, knowing that Solon didn't have room in his life for anything but the hunt.

Evening was upon them, but Althea insisted he leave right away. He was tired from the long time he'd spent out in the water and his sore back protested the idea of pulling a cart through the forest. Still, he turned and walked back into the palace, going to Althea's door. Pushing the beads aside, he found Althea waiting for him. She appeared paler than before he left and hobbled when she walked. It was clear that healing Cassandra had taken a lot out of the woman. Without saying a word, she motioned to the office.

Cassandra was still resting on the bed, her eyes closed. Only her chest moved, rising and falling with even breaths. Very gently, he lifted her up into his arms, cradling her light body to his chest. She hardly weighed more than a scrap of wool. He studied her face for signs of life, but she didn't move. Her eyelids didn't flutter, and she didn't moan in protest. Only the slight heat from her body and the shallow rise of her chest indicated she lived.

Carrying her from the office, he nodded at Althea who was now sitting wearily on the couch, a hand pressed to the side of her head.

"Heal her in small measures or you will drain yourself too quickly. Make sure you eat and feed her once she is strong enough to sit up. Until then, your health will nourish hers." Althea closed her eyes. "May the gods smile upon you for what you do, my lord."

"Thank you, Althea," Iason said. "Shall I send someone to you?"

"No," Althea denied. "I just need rest."

Iason carried Cassandra out of the palace. The sky had darkened and speckles of light started to move in the heavens. The sea's stars were drawn to the warmth of Ataran's magical dome and lit up the night. None could explain how they were blessed with night and day, only that it was the will of the god Poseidon when he cast them down into the ocean.

Making sure Cassandra's limbs were adjusted comfortably as he laid her in the cart, he covered her with several blankets. Then, facing forward, he lifted the cart's handles onto his shoulders. He didn't need to use his hands. The handles molded around his shoulders, hooking on. Slowly, he walked down the side of the hill. His back strained at the incline, but he didn't stop.

The city was quiet as he passed through. Iason had seen it many times and did not feel the need to look around. The homes were squished together forming whole city blocks with no alleys or inlets. They had no real windows, except for narrow slits along the wall. Not far from the palace was the marketplace. There was a large statue of a mermaid erected in the stone square, her long tail sweeping behind her naked upper body. The roads were paved with large stones, which made pulling the cart easy.

Shops were constructed in a circular pattern around the marketplace. Some sold readymade clothes; others sold baked goods, fish and other meats. Iason stopped. The shop owners lived behind their store fronts. Iason knocked first at the baker's, procuring flatbread. He did the same with the butcher, buying meat for the journey. Both men looked curiously at the cart.

"Mortal," Iason said softly, finding no reason to lie to them. Word of the successful hunt would soon spread and be rejoiced by all. "She's ill. I must take her to the countryside so she doesn't infect the other mortals."

"More mortal women, my lord?" they both asked in surprise.

"Aye, three total and two scylla," Iason answered, taking his items. "It was a good hunt."

"A very good hunt!" they exclaimed, louder than was prudent in the quiet morning hours.

Then, the butcher went on to inquire, "Do you seek suitors for her?"

"No. It is not known if she will live to accept suitors," Iason said. "I wouldn't want any to have hope only to be crushed when she passes eternally. And I do not want any overzealous men coming to my door before she is healed. The healer has ordered that her illness be contained first and foremost."

The butcher frowned but nodded that he understood.

Iason tried not to let the possessiveness show on his face. "There are the two others at the palace. Perhaps they will take suitors."

The words heartened the butcher somewhat and the man looked at the palace, smiling thoughtfully.

Iason's last stop was at the tailors. He bought long cloaks and simple gowns. The tailor lifted Cassandra's blankets and frowned at her thin frame.

"They will be too large on her," the tailor said, "but they are the smallest I have ready."

"I will take them. Thank you." Iason placed the bundle the tailor handed him in the cart next to Cassandra's leg.

Lifting the cart back on his shoulders, he pulled her through the quiet city streets into the surrounding forest. His home was near the borderlands, a three day walk from Atlas if he took his time, two if he jogged or walked fast without a break.

Trees grew high overhead. The forest was quiet, except for the occasional trill of a bird. The winged creatures were a rare beauty, one protected by law. When they were cast down into the ocean for angering the gods, some animals had survived. Some claimed the animals were immortal, while others claimed they'd seen them dead in the forest.

Iason stared at the path as he forced his legs to move. What was he doing? This was insanity. Still, despite his doubt, he kept moving, walking until his legs gave out and the exhaustion from the long hunt forced him to stop for the night.

Wearily, he looked at Cassandra. There was room in the cart, but it didn't feel right crawling in without her permission. Instead, he grabbed a spare cloak, wrapped it around his body and fell asleep on the hard ground.

The next morning, Iason broke his fast by eating as he pulled Cassandra onward. She hadn't moved all night, and, feeling sorry for her, he adjusted her limbs so they didn't get too weary from the same position. He turned her every once in a while, moving her onto one side and then the other in what he trusted was a comfortable position. Iason didn't know if his administrations helped, but it made him feel productive. Each time he touched her flesh, he let her have just a little bit of his energy. Hopefully, it was enough to get her by.

They didn't pass anyone in the forest, but he didn't expect to—not the route he traveled. That second night, he again slept on the ground, able to see the bright sea stars swimming overhead, framed by the branches of trees. Occasionally, the sea stars would part, letting a dark streak pass by. Iason knew it was only sea creatures disturbing them as it swam past.

The next morning, it looked as if Cassandra had moved her arms in her sleep. Though he couldn't be sure, that small sign gave him hope that she was getting better. He again ate, while continuing to haul the cart.

His body was stiffer than when he started due to the combination of being thrown into the hull of Cassandra's ship and the effort of carting her across the rough forest path. But he didn't stop. If he was to try and heal her, he didn't want to do it in the forest where Olympians might find him. He couldn't protect her in a weakened state.

Iason knew if he was to heal her at all, he had to get his strength up. The fast way to do so was either from sex or from swimming in his Merr form. Deciding on a swim, he took a winding path down a small salt pond.

Saltwater wasn't much good for bathing, but it

would allow him to stretch his muscles. Leaving Cassandra in the cart, he pulled off his clothes and dove into the briny waters. His body transformed, and he almost instantly felt better. His sore feet dissolved into a light tailfin. He stretched his arms, nearly weightless as he glided under the surface.

Iason flipped in circles, dove to skim his fingers along the bottom of the pond and stirred up dirt. He didn't need to come up for air, as his gills filtered the water so he could breath. By small degrees, his back felt better and his body renewed with life. Gliding beneath the surface, he couldn't help but contemplate his situation with Cassandra.

He was such a fool.

CHAPTER 8

CASSANDRA BLINKED. The first thing she saw was the dark sky. It didn't look like night, but it could have very well been evening. She heard a noise but didn't move as her body was rocked back and forth. The tops of trees passed overhead. Her limbs felt heavy, so heavy she couldn't lift them. Summoning her strength, she tilted her head up for a brief second. All she got was a glimpse of shoulder length blond hair fluttering in the breeze before she passed back into the tomb of darkness.

Next, when she awoke, the trees were no longer moving. There was no way to tell how much time had passed. A second? A week? Cassandra stared up at the sky. The stars seemed to dance in the heavens. It was a beautiful thing, but her swimming vision made her feel dizzy. She closed her eyes, pulling her arm up on her chest.

A loud yawn awoke her the third time. She felt rested, more so than she'd been in months. The pain was bad, and she wished she had her pain meds with her to help dull the deep ache. It was light out, but the sky was oddly dark. Maybe it was her vision. It was quite possible it was fading.

What had happened to the ocean? Where was she? Her mind didn't focus for long before it let the question slip from her thoughts. She stared at the sky, watching it with blurring eyes, getting lost in its blue depths.

Hearing movement, she looked around as her mind was drawn back to the present. She was in a wagon of some sort, surrounded by soft blankets. The situation was strange. But after the shock of being told she would be dead before she reached twenty five, nothing really fazed her anymore.

Some of her energy had returned, and she managed to lift her arm to the wooden side of the wagon. She weakly pulled herself up with trembling muscles. The first thing she noticed was a small pond, the light glistening on the water. Her eyes moved as she rested her chin on her hand. Movement caught her eye, and she stiffened.

A man dropped some sort of towel or garment off his body, and it was perhaps the most erotic thing she'd ever seen. He stood by the shore, naked, beautiful, tanned. The light hit him just right, contrasting every dip and curve of his muscular body. Not an ounce of fat marred him. He was like a Greek god, his body sculpted as if from a Renaissance artist's marble—so hard and perfect. Blond waves spilled over his shoulders. The locks looked a little tangled, but it added a wild appeal to his appearance. If she was hallucinating, Cassandra never wanted to be sane again.

Unable to help it, she stared at his firm ass. It dimpled as he walked toward the water. She forgot all about her pain as she watched him, curious as to who he was and what he was doing with her. He swung his arms to the side, stretching his back, twisting slightly at the waist. Cassandra's eyes widened as she saw his flaccid cock swing briefly into view. Even without an erection, the thing was bigger than any she'd seen—not that she'd seen many.

Something amazing happened when she watched him. She felt desire overriding the pain. Her heart skipped in her chest, and her body didn't feel as weak as before, but she knew she wasn't strong enough to pursue her feelings. She doubted she could even stand up for a long period of time, let alone summon the energy to touch him. Besides, she wasn't exactly looking her best these days.

Her breath caught in her chest as she watched him dive off the shore. His body moved with such elegance and grace. Cassandra was almost disappointed when he disappeared beneath the water's surface.

She watched for a long time for him to come up for air, but he didn't. Her arm grew tired, and she lowered herself back down. What if he was in trouble? What if the water was too shallow where he dived? Seeing a missing knot in the wood, she pushed the blanket aside and peeked out. If he drowned, wouldn't his body float to the top?

Suddenly, a large fin splashed up from the shore. Her heart nearly stopped in panic. The man was in trouble. There was something in the water with him.

Groaning, Cassandra pulled herself back up. Her limbs shook, and she cursed her weak body as she somehow managed to pull herself off the cart. She fell to the ground, so weak and tired, unable to stand.

Whoever this man was, she felt compelled to save him. She crawled on her hands and knees toward the shoreline. It was no use. Her willpower could only take her so far. She dropped on the ground, breathing heavily as she lay on her stomach. Her legs were tangled in thick folds of material, making it hard to move.

Cassandra watched, looking over the ground toward the lake. The hard earth pressed into her body, but she couldn't lift up. She used all her energy to keep her eyes on the water.

Please come up, she thought. *I can't save you. I can't...*

Cassandra gasped in relief when the man finally surfaced. His blond hair was slicked back against his head, clinging to his strong, muscled back. Fins were on the man's forearms. Then, he dipped over, swimming beneath the surface. His waist faded into a long green tail. The light reflected off his diamond shaped scales.

"Merman," she whispered in awe, the word so faint she wasn't sure if it came out or if she'd just thought it.

The man surfaced again, spinning around in the water to look at her. It was as if he heard her call. Cassandra didn't move. Even from the distance she could see the brilliant green of his eyes. She had green eyes, but she was sure hers had never sparkled like that—like two emeralds in the sunlight.

Cassandra's lids lowered over her gaze. She saw

him swim for her. His muscled arms pumped over the water, only to then pull his body onto shore. He didn't speak, but she heard a low voice in her head say, 'Cassandra?'

Was this a dream? Had her mind finally slipped? Was her body somewhere on the boat, locked to a bed, surrounded by ESC scientists trying to solve her dilemma with their logic and training? If there were scientists around, surely one of them would administer pain killers soon so she could enjoy this fantasy without the agony.

The merman used his arms to crawl onto the bank. His smooth, hairless chest was tanned like the rest of him. The fins on his forearms were green, a shade lighter than his emerald eyes and threaded with the soft whites and creams of a seashell. The skin of his forearm grew up around it. Gills fluttered before lying flat to his neck. Her heart fluttered like a butterfly in her chest, and she wished she could get up.

Silvery green scales dusted around his eyes, so light they were hardly noticeable. His legs were gone, as was all traces of his sex. In their place was a long silvery green tail. The caudal fin at the bottom unraveled as thin as wet silk. Her fingers flexed. She wanted to touch him. He looked beautiful, as if he were a god come from the ocean to rescue her.

A memory surfaced in her mind, the image of glittering green light in the darkness, of firm warm lips to hers, breathing into her, kissing her. Arms held her tight, so protective and secure. Coldness pulled at her, but the arms only held her tighter. She couldn't be on the boat. The boat had sunk into the ocean. That much she knew had been real.

Was it this man who had saved her from the dark and the cold? Was this life after death? Was this man taking her to the other side?

She watched him as he brushed the water from his tail. The scales transformed into flesh, replacing his tail with human legs. He stood, crossing the short distance to her. He was still naked, and she stared at his hips from beneath the narrowed slits of her eyes. Little trails of water beaded on his hard flesh, falling down over his body in little seductive rivulets.

If her mouth wasn't suddenly dry, she'd swallow in apprehension of his size. So big. Too big? His cock bounced as he moved, keeping her rapt attention until he came too close for her to see anything but his strong feet.

The man stopped before her, and she felt his

hand on her back. "What happened? What are you doing out of the cart?"

"Am I dead?" Cassandra whispered. She knew her words were faint, but the merman seemed to hear her just fine.

"You are sick." The man rolled her up into his arms. He touched her face and neck, the moisture left by his hands was pleasantly cooling.

Cassandra moaned, closing her eyes.

"Cassandra?"

She liked his voice. It was deep and rich. Looking at his face, she smiled. "My grandmother spoke of the ferryman, who would come to bring us to the other world when we died. Are you the ferryman taking me to cross the river of souls?"

"You are in a new world, but I am not a ferryman," he answered, smoothing back her hair with his damp palm. She felt a heat where his skin brushed hers, a spark of fire and light that went through her body. Her breathing deepened, and she moaned softly.

"Who are you?" she whispered, closing her eyes. Her body vibrated where he touched her, drawing from his heat. Cassandra could focus on little else.

"Iason the Hunter," he answered. "I'm taking care of you. I'm going to try and help you."

You hunt souls?

It took her a moment to realize she hadn't said the words aloud. When she opened her eyes again, he was putting her back into the cart. He eased her down gently, lying beside her. Cassandra reached up, caressing his neck, shivering at the coolness of his damp hair.

"Iason," she whispered, letting her fingers drop to her chest. "A soul hunter."

CHAPTER 9

Iason looked down at the woman beside him. How had she gotten out of the cart? He glanced around but could see no one else by the pond. Her hand glided over his cheek. He knew that she might still be suffering from the euphoria of being healed. It must be why she was calm about seeing him in his Merr form.

The swim had done much to energize him. Cassandra shivered, and he took her hand in his. Concentrating, he sent her his warmth and energy. She moaned, her lovely green eyes closing once more. Iason rubbed her arms, massaging them, before moving to her feet. He worked up her legs. Her skin was soft, and he found himself becoming aroused.

Iason knew that would happen. That is why

husbands only healed wives. The more he gave her of himself, the more he would want to claim her body. The closer he got to the point of climax, the more energy he could give her. The pleasure he would derive from sex would be more than enough energy to cure her—if done enough. The trick would be suffering to the furthest point only to deny himself in the end. He wanted her so much, but he would not take her without her consent.

Cassandra moaned, letting her thighs fall open to him. Iason tensed, his member so hard it wanted to explode. It was difficult to resist plunging in. She wiggled beneath him and her gown inched up over her thighs as she bent her knees. He let his hand glide up to her naked hip.

"So soft," he whispered. *I must heal her. I must heal her. Do not touch her in any other way.*

Cassandra's leg drew higher, teasing his naked waist with soft brushes of her skin to his. She pulled at her tunica's neckline, arching her back. Her lovely mouth opened, the bowed lips calling to him.

Iason tried to force his hands away. He drew them down to her thighs, ready to let go. Cassandra trapped his hand beneath hers, slowly she pulled it up her thigh only to take it further beneath her gown.

The tunica pulled up, revealing her naked sex. Cream glistened in the daylight. She wanted him.

He felt her ribs as she pulled his hand higher, only to stop at her soft breast. The nipple budded against his palm. Cassandra moaned. Iason jerked back, forcing control.

"We mustn't," he said. His body protested violently. Iason couldn't take her. Not like this. Not when she was sick, under his euphoric spell. Remembering his thoughts back in the palace—the idea that he would make her body his no matter what—he chuckled darkly. No matter how his body liked to tell him differently, his mind wanted her to be willing. He wanted her to want him, to know she wanted him.

When he again looked at her, Cassandra no longer moved. Knowing he couldn't keep staring at her exposed body, he pulled her dress down to cover her. Then, tucking her beneath the warm covers, he grabbed his tunic and went to the forest.

Hiding behind a tree, but still close enough to the cart that he could hear her if she needed him, Iason fisted his stiff erection. His dry palm was nowhere close to what he wanted, but it served to ease him of his affliction. It didn't take long. All he had to do was picture her wet, naked pussy surrounded by red curls and he was spilling his seed on the forest floor.

Afterward, he dressed and went back to the cart. Glancing over his shoulder, he frowned. She'd turned onto her side and was fast asleep. Her cheeks looked rosier than before and a soft smile curled her bowed lips.

Iason groaned as his cock twitched, eager to come back to life. Shaking his head, he lifted the cart onto his shoulders and began walking at a brisk pace into the forest.

"What have I gotten myself into?" he asked himself, swearing softly. "Saving her life is definitely going to kill me."

I am such a fool.

CHAPTER 10

CASSANDRA AWOKE FEELING BETTER than she had in months. Her body twinged with renewed life—so renewed in fact that she couldn't seem to stop thinking about sex. Or, more particularly, sex with the very hunky Iason the Hunter. He was the thing hot female fantasies were made of.

She watched his strong back as he pulled the cart. Though he was dressed, she could still see most of his body from beneath the gracefully draping tunic. It only fell to his upper thigh. His legs, arms and one shoulder were bare. Strong muscles bulged from what she could see of him. On his feet he wore leather strap sandals. His outfit only confirmed that she wasn't on Earth anymore. No one dressed like that. Leastways, not off the Florida coast where her ship had gone down.

Damn he was sexy!

Her libido must have kicked into overdrive because her sex nearly throbbed as moisture gathered between her legs. Her hand flexed, wanting to feel his muscles. Life was too short to hold back—or after-life, or whatever this place was.

Before she was diagnosed, she'd never been brave enough to come onto a man like Iason, let alone consider having sex with him. She would want to, but she would be too scared of what he would think of her. Was she pretty enough? Thin enough? Were her breasts too small? Now, as she stared death in the face—was perhaps already dead in some kind of in-between as Iason carted her to heaven or hell—she knew she wanted him. And, if he even gave the slightest indication he wanted her, she was deter-mined to go for it.

There was only one problem. She didn't have the energy for anything wild yet, or even tame for that matter, and she suspected she really needed to take a long bath. Leaning her head down, she sniffed. Yeah, she definitely needed a bath first.

Iason carted her toward a tall house. It was huge, with Romanesque columns holding up the roof over a long portico. It was one story tall and a cross between Ancient Roman architecture and an English manor house. The lawn was trimmed and the house well maintained. If she had to venture a guess, she would say it was made out of marble.

"Where are we?" she asked, praying that it wasn't her final destination. Her voice was hoarse from little use, but at least it was more than a whisper. "Is this a temple?"

Iason turned, looking surprised to see her awake. She forced a small smile for him. A moment passed as he stared at her. "My home."

Pleasure ran through her. His home? Cassandra bit her lip, allowing her eyes another glimpse of him as she stared at his tight backside. By the water, he'd been naked under his clothing. She wondered if he still was.

Was this heaven? Did she get a beautiful home and an even more beautiful god as her reward for a decent life lived? If so, they should put that into the description of the afterlife. With a picture of Iason next to the text, it would solve the crime problem. Everyone would want one. A twinge of pain hit her, and she moaned.

"Can you walk?" he asked, eyeing her as he came to the cart.

Cassandra wanted to say no but, remembering she needed a bath, she said, "Yes. I think so."

She shied away from him as she got out of the cart. The ground was hard against her bare feet, but she didn't mind. Iason grabbed a bundle from the cart as she made her way to the front steps. Holding onto a large Ionic column as she took the steps, she made it to the front door.

Columns reached up both sides, supporting the roof as it shaded the portico. The home was old but well taken care of. The house was unlocked. Iason opened the door, guiding her elbow as she walked in before him.

The front door led to a small entryway. Beyond that was a large atrium with marble walls and floors. Aside from a few benches, the atrium was barren. A hole was formed in the ceiling, letting fresh air into the house. Seeing a pool beneath the hole, she guessed it let in rainwater as well.

"For bathing," Iason offered, seeing her attention on the pool.

Cassandra pulled her arms close to her body, taking his words as a hint. Desperate to change the subject, she asked, "Do you live here alone?"

"No," he said.

Cassandra's heart nearly stopped beating. She

waited for him to tell her he was married. Could supernatural mermen soul hunters get married? The more she looked around, seeing how real everything felt, the more she began to lose faith in her theory of being dead. If she were dead, would she still feel sick?

"Feel free to go anywhere you like while you are here," Iason said. "My home is your home."

Naughtily, the only place she could think of wanting to go was his bedroom. Cassandra blushed. What was going on with her? She was like an animal in heat, ready to hump the first thing that walked by. Okay, well it did help that the first thing that walked by was a Greek god.

He crossed the hall and opened a small door. "For personal needs."

Cassandra looked, seeing what could only be a restroom. She nodded, and he shut the door. Beyond the atrium, she saw an indoor garden. The sweet scent of nature filled the air, and she smiled softly. Glancing at him, she said, "Your home is beautiful."

He nodded once, looked like he wanted to say something and then held back. He gave her thin frame a once over. "I'm supposed to feed you when you can sit up by yourself."

Cassandra glanced down. Oddly, she wasn't

hungry. "I would like a bath, if it's not too much trouble."

Iason nodded. He looked down at the bathing pool and then back at her. "Should I...?"

Okay, that offer was just too much. The idea of him bathing her was very tempting. Her smell wasn't. Cassandra felt weak but lied, "I'm fine. I can do it."

"Wait here. I will get you soaps." Iason took off into a side door.

Cassandra walked over to a door, her feet shuffling. She looked at the indoor garden on the other side. Stone paths wound through the bushes and trees, lined with stone benches. There was a thin roof overhead. It let in enough light to help the plants grow, without letting the delicate blossoms overheat. A cooler breeze swept in from an opened door. The air was sweet with the smell of berries and flowers. It was so pretty and well-tended. She wondered who took care of it.

"Ready?"

Cassandra jolted in surprise at his voice. She nodded. Glancing around the atrium with its many doors, she asked, "Will anyone come in?"

"No. The caretakers are away traveling and won't be back any time soon. It is only the two of us. I will be in the kitchen preparing food." Iason set a towel and jars down by the pool. "When there is company, we draw water from the pool and heat it in pipes before taking it to a tub. Unfortunately, the pool has not been in use and water is not heated in the pipes."

"It is fine." Cassandra assured him. "Thank you."

Was he nervous? Why wasn't he looking at her? She watched his throat work.

"The small jar is for your mouth," he said, clearing his throat as he turned quickly away. "I will be in the kitchen if you need me."

Cassandra chuckled to herself. He was acting strangely. Looking around the atrium, she figured it was no stranger than her situation.

Slipping out of her clothes, she gently stepped down into the pool. She wondered why she wasn't freaking out more. She was in a strange place with a strange, albeit very handsome, merman. But, the truth was, she couldn't force herself to think about her situation. It was like a cloud was over her thoughts and if she concentrated too hard the cloud only thickened.

Cassandra wished the water was warmer but wasn't about to complain. He had warned her it wouldn't be heated. She kept a sharp eye on the doors as she picked up a jar. Sniffing the contents, she was pleasantly surprised to find it was like lavender mint. By its consistency she decided it was soap. Cassandra washed her hair and body with it. Her skin tingled with a pleasing warmth.

The next jar was creamier, and she used it as a conditioner. It worked beautifully, and she was sure her hair had never been so silky soft in all her life. Lastly, she brushed her teeth with her finger, rinsing with a glass of water he'd left for her. She watched, seeing how the pool seemed to filter itself. Almost immediately the soap from her hair dissipated from the water.

Liking the weightless feel of being suspended in water, Cassandra laid her back along the pool's edge. She closed her eyes, content for the moment to just relax.

CHAPTER 11

IASON CHOPPED the piece of auv fruit like a madman, blindly hacking into it with his knife so that bits of sticky pulp flew up with each knife stroke. Did her voice have to be so sultry? He knew he'd been babbling as he left her to bathe, but he'd been so distracted with imagined scenes of her in the tub, her hands soaping up her breasts, the water surrounding her, that he'd barely been able to concentrate. Hopefully, she hadn't noticed.

Glancing down, he stopped hacking into the fruit long enough to frown. Holding his hands to the side, he looked down his body. He was erect. Again.

Iason growled and chopped harder, puréeing the fruit into a liquid pile of slush as he worked out his sexual frustrations. Althea had no idea what she had asked him to do, or how difficult it was going to be for him. He knew Cassandra was not well yet, that she could very well slip back into unconsciousness. In fact, Althea had said it was better if she didn't awaken because of the amount of pain she was in.

The healer had been right when she said Cassandra was very sick. He felt an ache in his bones even now. How she put up with so much pain, he couldn't imagine. He'd only taken a measure of it and he was on the verge of complaining. Cassandra hadn't said a damn word about it, and, if anyone had a right to complain, it was that woman.

As she'd stood in the atrium, Cassandra had swayed slightly on her feet. He took a deep breath and set down the knife, worried. Maybe he shouldn't have left her alone in the tub. What if she drowned? What if she needed him and he couldn't hear her?

He should check on her.

For her health, he should check on her.

It was the right, gentlemanly thing to do.

Iason nodded, his decision made. Hurrying to the atrium to check on her, he stiffened to see her unmoving in the water. Her head was tilted back against the edge, but it looked as if she would slip under any second. He rushed to her side, mindlessly going down the steps into the pool, as he said her name. "Cassandra? Cassandra, are you all right? Wake up."

He was halfway in the water when her eyes flew open to him. Her thin arms covered her breasts as she stood. Automatically, he looked at her body.

By All the Gods!

"I thought you were hurt," he said, trying to force his eyes from the thatch of curls between her thighs. It was impossible. He knew he stared, but he couldn't turn away. She was very... naked. And wet. And, oh, her sex had been so ready for him in the cart.

"I'm feeling much better," Cassandra said. Her sultry tone wrapped around him, stirring his already thick blood.

To his surprise, she dropped her arms from her breasts, exposing them to him. Iason continued to stare. If not for the nervous way she bit her lip, he thought she might be unaware of her actions.

She let him look at her, standing tall as he did just that. Iason was torn between kissing her pouty mouth, sucking that lip from between her teeth, and forcing himself to leave her alone. His eyes dipped down once more to the thatch of curls. Even in his mortal years he was sure he'd never seen a woman's nether hair quite that color. It was exotic, like the tiny flowers that bloomed in the deepest parts of the Abyss.

Iason waited for her to make a move. What was she doing? What was she waiting for? Should he touch her? Was this show an invitation? Or did he leave her to tend to his affliction with his own hand like he'd been doing?

She tilted her head to the side, her lips parted, her green eyes staring at him. She looked so innocent, so fragile. He felt like the beast come to ravish her. Iason swallowed, more than ready to play the part.

Licking his lips, he couldn't help but think, *I am such a fool.*

CHAPTER 12

Cassandra took a deep breath. She didn't know much, but she knew she wanted to be with Iason. Her body burned for contact. It had been too long since someone held her, touched her, made love to her. She needed to be touched, to know she could still feel something other than pain. Only problem was, she'd never played the role of the seductress before and was a little daunted on where to begin.

Iason made a move to leave her alone in the bath. Seeing he wasn't going to take initiative, she asked, "Am I dead?"

At that a slight smile curled his firm lips. He turned back to her. His eyes kept glancing down her body. It was clear he wasn't completely immune to her. The idea gave her hope.

"No," he answered.

Once her mind had become clearer, she'd guessed as much. "Did you pull me from the water?"

"Aye." Iason's gaze again dipped down to her breasts. She didn't bother to cover them. He licked his lips before turning his eyes away. There was something sexually freeing about being so bold.

"Are we on some sort of secret island?" Why had he stopped looking at her? She knew she was too thin, but wasn't he even the least bit interested in fucking her? Looking down his muscular form, she relaxed some. She could see the telltale bulge of an erection beneath his short toga.

Oh, yeah, he was definitely interested. Her body stirred. The strange euphoric cloud was over her senses until she was focused on one thing—seducing Iason.

"Aye." His gaze flickered to hers once more, and he cleared his throat. "Ataran."

"And you are a merman?"

"Aye." He visibly tensed, no doubt waiting for her to scream.

Cassandra wasn't too alarmed by the fact. Her grandmother had always told her that such things as witches and the supernatural existed. Once, Cassandra was even convinced she'd seen a ghost. So why would a handsome merman upset her? The human legends must have come from somewhere, and, unlike the ESC scientists, she didn't put stock in the logical explanation for everything. There was too much that modern thinking couldn't explain—like the tingling one got on the back of the neck when a ghost was near, or how a mother could feel her child needed her from across town. Why not a few sexy mermen living in a tropical paradise on some uncharted island?

Cassandra glanced down at his legs in the water, furrowing her brow in confusion. He shrugged and explained, "This is fresh water. My body changes in salt."

Cassandra laughed softly at his sheepish look. It was as if he waited for some big freak-out reaction from her.

"Then I just have one last question for the time being," she said, studying his eyes to see if he would lie to her. He nodded once for her to go ahead. "Did you cause our ship to wreck?"

"No. We were hunting the scylla. It wrecked your ship. You humans caught my friend Caderyn in a net while we were trying to capture the creature." Iason didn't once glance away. "We tried to stop the wreck but were too late."

Cassandra nodded, sensing that he wasn't lying to her. He turned to leave. She reached for his arm, wanting to touch him. "Wait."

He stared at her hand on his arm.

"I want to thank you for saving me," she said. It was half true. It would have been less painful in the long run to have died in the ocean, but he didn't know that. Besides, if she had died, she wouldn't be on a tropical isle with an incredibly handsome merman. Having seen him naked firsthand, she knew he was shaped like a human male and most likely capable of great things when it came to sex.

Cassandra moved in front of him, stepping up on the underwater stairs so she was more at his level. A moment of weakness swept through her, but she ignored it. She refused to get sick now. Not now. She wanted to feel all life had to offer, all Iason had to offer. Her life was too short to take things slowly. Besides, the plus of her condition was that she didn't have to worry about disease. She wouldn't be around long enough for anything to be a problem. As far as pregnancy, the doctors had mentioned it wasn't possible. Cassandra had been upset, but it was all for the best. It would be much harder going, knowing she left a baby behind without a mother.

Cassandra closed her eyes, determined not to

think about anything sad. She'd grieved enough. Now was the time to enjoy.

"You don't have to do this." Iason whispered. Despite his words, he didn't back away, and he didn't stop her as she slid her hands to the material knotted over one shoulder. She pushed the material off his arm, baring his chest.

"Let me bathe you," she said, running her palms over his smooth chest. Bathing him was just an excuse to explore his body. He didn't appear dirty, and he smelled fresh and clean. "You must be tired from carting me around."

Cassandra backed up, trying to force her heartbeat to slow. It didn't do any good. She wanted this, but she was still nervous. She took up the jar of soap and dipped her fingers in. Working a lather between her palms, she came back to him.

The soap felt like silk between their flesh as she slowly washed him. He was so strong, so rock hard. Cassandra had never felt anything like it. She took her time, exploring each curve, caressing her fingers over his taut chest, back, and arms.

Iason didn't move to encourage or dissuade her so she kept going. In fact, he didn't move at all, save to take long, deep breaths. Her hands continued to move over his form, unconsciously testing the firmness of his tight body. The texture of his skin fascinated her, as did the gentle slopes of his bulging muscles. With each touch, it was like she could feel her body connecting to his. Her nerve endings jumped beneath her skin like little firecracker explosions.

Cassandra's lips parted. She wanted to kiss him, to taste him, but she refused to rush things. His clothes still hung about his waist, hiding his firm backside from view. Working her way around to the front, she met his emerald eyes. "Wet your hair."

Iason kneeled before her, not stepping back. He parted his lips as they passed inches away from her breasts. She felt him blowing against her skin, causing her nipples to jump into two very erect points. It was a gentle, seductive caress she felt all the way to her toes. He continued to blow, ruffling the curls between her thighs. With their marble surroundings, it was very easy to imagine she was the innocent maiden being forced to service the big, bad Roman gladiator.

He dipped beneath the water. When he came up, he stayed on his knees, his eyes boring into her sex. Cassandra reached behind her back, blindly fumbling for the soap. Her fingers shook as she lathered his hair for him and ordered him to rinse. He obeyed.

She smiled. Maybe she wasn't the innocent maiden in this scenario. Maybe she could be the rich noblewoman in control of her new gladiator slave. The idea of being able to command such a man, to dominate him, made her knees weak with pleasure.

Cassandra put the conditioner in his hair and pushed at his head. He obligingly went under the water once more. She ran her fingers through the silky locks before letting him up. When he came up from the water, he stood before her, again blowing at her flesh. His wet clothing hugged his waist, clinging to his upper thighs.

A strand of wet hair plastered over one of his eyes. The blond looked darker now that it was wet. She ran her fingers through his hair, pushing it back from his face. Her nipples grazed his hot flesh and her breath caught at the very heat of him, as stinging nerves sent a shockwave down her body.

Cassandra met his eyes as she pulled the cloth belt at his waist. The material adhered to his skin, and she tugged at the edges, pulling it back until it fell heavily into the water. She looked down. His cock was full, and it was arousing just knowing she'd done that to him. She sucked on her bottom lip, unconsciously biting it.

His groin was free from hair and his legs had very little. The mushroom shaped tip looked ready to conquer. Veins ran up the sides of his smooth shaft, a shaft so thick and tall she was unsure whether or not it would actually fit inside her. Despite this rather girly fear, she felt her body already getting wet as it was more than willing to try.

She got more soap and glided her hands over him once more. Rubbing in long strokes, she moved around him, kneeling into the pool as she cleaned his legs. At her gentle push, he lifted his feet from the water.

There was freedom in knowing she had nothing to lose. Taking her hands, she ran them over his hips, reaching around to his pelvic area. He tensed, his breath catching as her fingers missed his erect cock and slid back around to grab his ass. His head tipped back, and she felt him quiver.

Boldly, she ran her soapy hand along his cheeks and inner thighs, washing him most intimately. The first sound since they'd started this game left his throat in a long, low growl. His entire length tensed as hard muscles strained beneath his skin.

Cassandra let her fingers glide forward to soap

his balls from underneath, pressing her thumb to the very sensitive piece of flesh buried between his balls and his ass. Taking her free hand, she reached around and soaped his cock. She had to twist to clean all of it because it was too big for her hand to close around.

Cassandra bit her lip and thought, *Thank goodness I read all those erotic novels in college.*

How else would she have gotten ideas like this? How else would she know that the flesh buried beneath a man's balls was a bundle of nerves? Or that if she pulled down firmly on his testicles she could stop him from coming and make his erection last longer? It wasn't as if that conversation ever came up in sex education class.

His hips worked against her hand as she masturbated him. In that moment, she knew the big hunter was helpless against her power over him. Never did she think she'd become so aroused just by giving a man pleasure.

Already her pussy was tight. Her clit tingled. It was like she could feel his orgasm approaching inside of her. As tension built in him, it built in her. She leaned over and bit the side of his ass cheek. He jerked. She did it again, her tongue bathing the firm mound of muscled flesh with short little licks.

"Cassandra," he groaned. She liked that he knew who touched him, liked the way her name sounded as he cried out in pleasure, thrusting and grunting against her hand. "Cassandra!"

"Come for me," she commanded him, squeezing his shaft and his balls at the same time. His ass tensed, working back and forth beautifully. "Now."

To her amazement, Iason was able to obey, coming on her command. His body jerked, and she felt his hot semen flowing over the back of her hand like lava.

Cassandra felt as if her body exploded just a little to join him in his release. It was like she was possessed, mad with sexual power. Her scalp tingled as if she'd been shocked with electricity. She pulled her hands back, slowly washing them off. His knees wobbled as he dipped down into the water to rinse. Her legs were a little unsteady as well, but she managed to stand upright.

"Cassandra," he began, his words a pleasured growl. Lids drooped lazily over his eyes, and when he looked up at her it was with the sated expression of a wild beast—tempered for the moment yet still hot beneath the surface.

"Shh," she ordered, feeling giddy. "I didn't give you permission to speak."

Iason quirked a brow. "I do not need your permission."

Cassandra shivered. Mm, good, he was going to be defiant. This was going to be so much fun. "You do if you want to come again."

Understanding dawned on his face, and he slowly bowed his head. "My lady."

Cassandra shivered, liking the title he bestowed upon her. She thought about going to the gardens and making him pleasure her with his mouth while surrounded by the sweet smell of fresh berries or flowers or whatever plants those were in there, but a bed sounded too comfortable to pass up. "That's a good little slave. Now, lead me to your bedroom."

Iason stood and stepped from the water, his head turning to watch her as his eyes smoldered with passion. Cassandra followed him to one of the doors, watching his tight ass as he walked. She took a deep breath and then another.

Was she really doing this?

Was she really going to have sex with Iason?

Yes. Cassandra took a calming breath. Yes, she most certainly was.

She was pleased to find the room clean and the bed large. The décor was simple. It had cream colored walls, accented with red and gold. There was a bronze vase in the corner, a round table and a wardrobe. A crimson red comforter lay on the large bed. It was embroidered with a giant sun pattern. Frescos were painted on the top half of the walls. They formed perfect rectangles around the room. Most of them were of ancient landscapes. Drawn to the bed, she lay down on the comforter. The mattress was soft, and she stretched out on it.

"I see you are feeling better," Iason said, coming to the end of the bed. His cock was at half mast, and he made no move to cover himself from her eyes. She liked his confidence. He was completely unembarrassed by his nakedness, not that he had reason to be otherwise.

"I want you to kiss me," Cassandra said, rubbing her body so he could watch.

Iason crawled onto the bed, keeping their bodies parted as he moved over her. She forced her hands over her head, not touching him. He leaned down, lightly licking her mouth with his tongue, flicking it back and forth. "You kissed me in the water with your tongue. I liked it."

Cassandra moaned, sucking his tongue between her lips. His mouth was so warm, tasted so sweet, like wine. Iason deepened the kiss, letting her suck his lips down to hers. A small noise left her throat as he thoroughly conquered her mouth. Gasping for breath, she had to pull away first. He smiled. It was a knowing, victorious expression.

"Kiss me again," she ordered, purposefully hardening her tone as she struggled to keep from gasping for breath. Her heart beat so fast she could hear it in her ears, feel it trying to jump out of her chest. When he leaned down to take her mouth, she shook her head. She drew her knees up and said, "Kiss me down here."

The look on his face was priceless. At first it was absolute confusion, as he looked down at her parted thighs, before turning to utter curiosity. He crawled down her body, motioning between her thighs in question. "Here?"

"Mm, yes," Cassandra said, parting her legs a little wider. She clenched her teeth, almost scared he would laugh at her boldness. Her body was tense as she waited for his response.

Iason looked down at her body for so long she felt heat flooding her cheeks. Just when she was about to lose her nerve and call the game off, he slowly leaned down, angling his head so that he approached her folds like they were a pair of lips. He brushed his mouth softly to her, before pulling back, hesitating as he angled his head one direction only to turn it to the other.

Cassandra watched in amazement. The poor, gorgeous man looked utterly and completely confused. Was it possible that he'd never...?

Cassandra's whole body jerked with excitement even as she choked back a laugh of surprise. "Have you kissed a woman like that before?"

Iason looked at her, shaking his head once. He licked his lips. His green eyes practically sparked with intensity. In that instant, she knew he would be up to the challenge.

Cassandra reached between her thighs and parted her sex for him. Her voice soft, she said, "Kiss me."

He obeyed, softly moving his lips against her. Cassandra moaned. He was so gentle it was almost torture. When he pulled back he licked her cream from his lips. A sound of pleasure left his throat, and he murmured, "So good."

Iason eagerly went down for more. Cassandra gasped at how easily he caught on. Aggressively he drank from her body, licking and sucking every inch of her slit. His nose pressed up at her fingers until she realized he wanted her to let go. Breathing hard, he leaned back to study her intently. He pulled on her thighs, readjusting her hips on the bed for a better angle.

"I want to taste how you come," he said.

Cassandra's whole body jerked at the words, and she realized that she was no longer in control, if she ever had been. Iason was like the hunting predator, waiting for the prey to get comfortable before showing his full strength.

Cassandra didn't care. Control had been great, but if being controlled came with perks like this, she was more than willing to sign on. Iason learned fast, adjusting speed and pressure with the jerks of her body and sounds of her moans. Soon he was sucking her clit like a pro.

"Come for me," he said, repeating her words from earlier. The commanding tone rocked through her. He growled, slipping a thick finger up into her. His hand rocked naturally against her body. "Come for me, Cassandra. Come for me now. I want to taste it."

How could she refuse? Her body tensed as she swung a thigh around his head, burying him in her pussy. He groaned loud and long, vibrating her. She came, rocking and jerking in her climax.

Iason didn't stop until her leg fell weakly to the

side. Breathing hard, she looked at him in amazement. "You were lying. You've done that before."

"No," he said, and she read the truth of it in his eyes. "But I will be doing it much more often."

A strange feeling came over her at the thought. A man like Iason wouldn't be without feminine company.

"Do you have many lovers?" she asked, still trying to slow her heart beat. "I mean, not ever, but at the moment. I mean, right now? Not right this second, but do you have...?"

Cassandra's words trailed off as she became unable to complete the sentence. Her stomach tensed as she waited for his answer. Part of her wanted to crawl back on the bed and hide, though it was stupid after what they'd already done. He lounged between her thighs as if it was the most natural place to be, licking his lips and touching her body in light strokes —not just her sex, but her legs and stomach.

Absently, he said, "No. I don't have many lovers at this moment, right now."

"How many?" she insisted, wondering why she was torturing herself. She had no right to ask him that.

Iason glanced meaningfully over her body, before looking her right in the eye. "One."

Cassandra blushed. She felt the heat rising up her throat. It was the curse of being so fair complexioned that her face showed every slight embarrassment as a bright pink beacon shining on her face.

"And you? How many lovers do you have right now, at this moment?" He turned back to her legs, skating his fingers over her thighs in absent patterns.

Cassandra shrugged and shook her head in denial, simply stating, "You."

Iason growled, coming up her body. His hand stroked boldly up her ribs to a breast. Kissing her, he whispered against her mouth, "This pleases me greatly, Cassandra."

She couldn't breathe. There was no way this could be real.

Please, no one wake me up. I don't want to leave this perfect dream. Just let me drown in it.

CHAPTER 13

Iason lay over Cassandra's naked body. His thighs straddled hers as he kissed her. He couldn't believe how wonderful her flavor had been. He could have drunk of it forever. It was definitely something he would be doing again.

Cassandra whimpered at his light kiss, and he felt her body stirring. Energy flowed out of him, into her, and back again. She needed his whole body, and he was more than willing to give it to her, even if it killed him.

At first, when she touched him, he'd concentrated on healing her, of giving her his strength. However, it turned out he didn't need to concentrate. If her body wanted it, his body wanted to give it to her. He'd let her suck him dry of all his life force if she wanted. Before, he'd thought there were only a few ways for Merr to die. Now he knew of another, a more pleasurable way. He could be drained by the beauty before him. If he had to choose his death, he couldn't think of a better way to go.

A rush of warmth left him, spreading out over her. His flesh became sensitive to the touch, and he felt every place she pressed into his body. Her nipples hardened against him, just as his erect shaft tightened and hardened against her. She wiggled again, and he nearly groaned at the feel of her soft stomach pressing up against his erection. Not once did he stop to think about not finishing what they had started.

In the bath, he couldn't believe how she'd wanted him. It was as if their being together was natural. She touched him like no other had touched him, giving completely as she stroked his shaft to release. He'd thought only to play with her this night so that she may heal, to do everything but put his cock inside her. But, after tasting with his mouth and feeling her tight sheath on his finger, he knew there was no stopping it. He was going to make love to her.

There was so much that hadn't been said with words, but Iason trusted the gods knew what they were doing. They blessed him with her, sent her to him from the surface world. He felt it at the first touch, when she'd grabbed him and kissed him beneath the ocean waves. Cassandra was his gift from the god of the sea. Poseidon had blessed him, after all these long, long years.

Why shouldn't the gods bless him? He'd paid the price for his people's vanity. He'd honored them the best he could. Maybe the women were Poseidon's way of saying he would someday forgive them for what they'd done and let them return to the world of sunlight. It was what the Merr wanted, because that's what they'd always wanted since being cast down, but Iason wondered if, once they reached the surface world, they would miss the underwater one.

"Let me make love to you," he said, kissing along her throat.

"Isn't that what we've been doing?" she asked, sounding hesitant.

"We've been playing. I wish to do more," Iason answered. He stopped her words as he showed her with his kiss how much he desired her. When he pulled back, she was moaning. "Tell me to take you."

"Yes," she breathed, not looking at him. "Take me."

Iason captured her nipple, suctioning his mouth

to her breasts as he sucked it, swirling his tongue in small circles over the tip. She gasped, instantly jerking, and he grinned at having found yet another use for the suctioning kiss that had saved her life. Her fingers clawed his shoulders, scratching him. The tiny bit of pain felt good, making his skin more alive. He sensed the need in her to be controlled.

"Turn over," he commanded her softly, "and part your legs. I want to touch you."

Iason was a man used to being listened to and was pleased when she maneuvered her body, slipping her legs outside of his, he grinned. Bracing his thighs between hers, he pushed her legs further apart. Cassandra moaned lightly. He massaged along her spine, running his fingers over her petite backside. He pulled her cheeks apart as he massaged, getting peeks of her glistening sex.

He took it slowly, even as his own body urged him to hurry. He kissed her back, moving lower to bathe her butt with tiny licks as she'd done to him in the bath. She jerked, arching up. Iason pressed her lower back gently, forcing her to rest against the mattress.

Taking a finger, he rubbed her soft folds from behind, keeping her legs parted wide with his thighs.

When she was squirming for more, trying to thrust back onto his hand, he pushed a finger into her, stretching her body. Cassandra moaned, again trying to get up as he moved his hand away.

Iason came over her, pushing her hair aside as he kissed the back of her neck. His cock nestled against the cleft of her ass. She shivered at the light touch, and he watched as little bumps formed over her flesh. Bracing his weight on his elbows, he lay against her body, letting his heat warm her. His hands rested against her arms. His cheek pressed close to her ear, trapping her down but not hurting her. He nipped the lobe, biting and licking it tenderly.

"Please," Cassandra gasped. She pushed her butt up, angling her body in acceptance. "Iason, please."

Iason groaned. He pulled back, running his hands down her sides before drawing her hips up so she was on her hands and knees before him. When she stayed like that, offering her body to him, he took his cock and dragged the tip over her wet slit. It felt glorious—so wet, so sweet, so ready and accepting.

"Like this?" he asked, pressing slightly against her. "Is this how you want it?"

"Yes," she sighed. "Any way you want, just please, hurry. I need you."

MICHELLE M. PILLOW

Iason groaned, liking her confidence, the way she boldly said and did what she wanted. These were great qualities in a lover, not that he really remembered what it was like to have a lover. It had been so long since he'd made love to a woman. He wanted to savor every moment.

A soft light came from above, peeking through little holes in the ceiling. Even so, the room was dim. There was enough light to see by, but it was dark enough to be romantic.

Cassandra's body was tight as he probed her with his cock, clamping down on him. He withdrew several times, and she could tell he was trying not to hurt her as he stretched her passage to fit him. It was agonizingly sweet torture. He worked deeper and deeper, and already she felt the pleasure of tension building. Iason took his time, moving so slow and gentle.

It was erotic to be before him like this, on her hands and knees, taking what he gave her. Cassandra gasped. He was so big, so powerful. She knew that women weren't supposed to *want* to be conquered

122

and taken in this day and age of political correctness and equal rights, but she didn't care. She wanted him to ride her, control her, fuck her. Men were men, women were women, and she liked the feeling of being taken care of.

She had nothing to lose. Every moment was precious. Besides, it felt too damned good.

Reaching between them, she pressed her arm along her clit as she wrapped her fingers around the base of his shaft. Iason groaned, sounding almost frustrated as he tried to go deeper. Knowing it had been so long and her body might be too tight to take him all in, she let her hand compensate for his extra length. He moaned in approval and pulled out of her. The cream from her body moistened her hand as his shaft passed through.

As he thrust forward, increasing his speed, she had the pleasure of her arm bouncing against her clit. Iason rubbed her ass cheeks, massaging them, before wetting a finger in her cream. His hips worked his body into hers, taking her hand and her pussy at the same time. Cassandra moaned. A wet finger ran along her cleft, circling the tight rosette of her ass. No man had ever touched her there, and she waited for him to thrust his finger inside. He didn't. Instead, he merely touched her, rubbing along her body as he thrust harder and harder.

The probing finger felt so wicked, the invitation of what more could come if she only begged it of him. Cassandra wanted all of it, all of him, but could she say the words aloud? When he touched her like this, she didn't feel sick, didn't think of dying.

How could she when she felt so alive? So wonderful?

An orgasm hit her, rocking her to the core, causing her pussy to clench. Her fingers contracted as her sex spasmed and squeezed Iason tight. He grunted, pulling her hips back so hard that he bypassed her hand and slid deeper. His groan echoed over her, and she felt the erratic jerks of his body as he came.

Afterward, he let her go. His body slid out of her as she collapsed on the bed. Iason was instantly at her side, absently rubbing her back. She felt a strange vibrating warmth over her lower stomach, taking away any discomfort she felt at his size.

"You are so small," Iason said. "Did I hurt you?"

Cassandra turned her face to look at him. He studied her, his green eyes searching hers. She was again struck by the sheer depth of their color. She leaned over, kissing him gently, before saying, "Mm, no. I'm just sleepy."

Iason nodded. The bedcovers had gotten messed up during their lovemaking, and he pulled them out from under her legs. Covering her, he pulled her into his arms and said, "Then go to sleep."

CHAPTER 14

WHEN CASSANDRA AWOKE from a restful sleep, Iason was gone. She frowned but felt better than she had in ages. This must be one of those 'good days' the doctors told her about. Stretching, she blushed just to think about what she'd done. She had no regrets, but it was rather bold.

Sliding out of bed, she saw a long, loose dress over the end. Knowing it must be for her, she pulled it over her head. Her body was thin, and it hung over her frame. The gown was made out of plain blue wool, not her most flattering color, but it was warm. It was one solid piece with a seam running straight down the front. A belt was with it, and she knotted it loosely around her waist, letting the ends drape. She wondered what had happened to the exercise pants and tank top she'd been wearing. The sandals on the floor were a little big, but she put them on anyway.

As she was heading out of the door, Iason was coming in. Coming face to chest with him, she blushed anew. He smelled wonderful. Her eyes moved up to his as he took the first step back. He was holding a tray of food. Cassandra's stomach growled, and she realized she had an appetite. In fact, she was starving.

"I was going to bring this to you," he said. "Are you well enough to be up?"

Cassandra gave him a weird look. There was no way he could know about her illness. Then she giggled. He was talking about his size stretching her and... She couldn't finish the thought with him standing there looking at her expectantly. Her voice a squeak, she said, "No, no, I'm fine. Good. Fine. Better than fine. Good."

"Then shall we take this to the dining room instead?" He motioned toward the garden.

Cassandra nodded, trying to find her composure. When he turned, she quickly fussed with her hair, combing it back with her fingers before pinching her cheeks to get some color into them. She wished she had some makeup to put on, knowing she must look frightfully pale. Her eyes drifted down over Iason's body as she smoothed her hair. He again wore a short tunic that came to mid-thigh. She found herself staring at his butt.

Iason glanced back at her, and she quickly dropped her eyes and smiled innocently. He quirked a brow in amusement and again turned to watch where he was going. Cassandra made a face, more at herself than at him, and stole another quick glance down.

He led her over the winding stone paths of the enclosed gardens, past the delicate flowers and sturdier shrubbery. A cooler breeze swept in from an opened door, and she caught a glimpse of the forest in the distance. The air was sweet with the smell of nature.

Beyond the garden was the dining room. Cassandra glanced around, surprised to see a low table on the floor. Iason set the tray down and motioned for her to take a seat. There were no chairs, only large rectangular pillows. She gingerly sat down on one, sinking into its voluptuous depths.

"Eat. I will get wine," he said, turning to go back through the gardens.

Cassandra waited until he was gone before attacking the large tray. She was starved. Taking several of the berries that acted like garnish, she popped one in her mouth. They were delicious and tasted like blueberries.

Intermingled with the blueberries were large pink fruit slices that had a salty sweet flavor to them and were extra juicy. She took a big bite, glancing out into the gardens. The last thing she wanted was Iason seeing her eating like a pig at the trough.

Seeing a bowl of green paste, she lifted it and smelled. It reminded her of cheese, but the green color turned her away from it. Taking a warm flat-bread, she studied the meat in the middle of the tray. It was fish, if she had her guess, chopped into cubes. Picking one up, she sniffed it before taking a small bite. It was delicious. The herbs on it were perfect, almost like rosemary with a hint of mint.

Nearly moaning, she stuffed several into her mouth, chewing happily. The food was so good that she didn't see Iason coming back until it was too late. Her cheeks were puffed out with fish and berries when she heard him clear his throat.

Cassandra froze, unable to meet his eyes as she tried to swallow the big bite. The action wasn't as delicate or as subtle as she'd hoped, and she ended up coughing violently. Iason was at her side in an instant, setting a wine pitcher down on the table. He rubbed her back soothingly saying, "Easy."

Cassandra shrugged him off, caught between laughing and choking. When she could breathe, she said, "I'm good, thanks."

"Afraid I would eat it all when I got back?" he teased.

Cassandra laughed, giving him a properly embarrassed look. "Sorry. It was so good I couldn't resist. I started and couldn't stop. It feels like an eternity since I ate anything."

And felt well enough to be able to keep it down, she added silently.

Iason laughed and moved over across from her. He lounged over on his side, relaxing as he grabbed a berry. Tossing it into his mouth, he gave her a sultry look as he chewed. The short toga showed off his strong thighs. It was hard not to stare, but she somehow managed.

Having sex was one thing, having him look at her like they'd just had sex was another completely. Her mind racing to ease the silence, she asked, "So, mermen, huh?"

"You are fine with this. Why?" The teasing look faded into seriousness.

"Would you feel better if I started screaming and running around? Because I can if you would like me to." Cassandra winked.

"Are most women like you where you come from? Would they accept this about me?" Iason popped another berry in his mouth. Watching his lips move was definitely a lesson in seduction all on its own.

"No, probably not," she admitted. "I think I'm all right with it because my grandmother believed in the supernatural. She passed the belief onto me. When she died, I was sure I saw her spirit come to visit me. She touched my head, and I could almost feel her. She told me that everything was going to be all right and not to worry about anything that might happen. She told me to accept my fate and..."

"And?"

"Nothing," Cassandra lied. Her grandmother had told her to live to the fullest and to have faith in what could not be reasoned. It was like she'd been warning her about what was to come. Within a year, Cassandra had been diagnosed.

"What is the supernatural in your world?"

"Um, ghosts, spirits, magic, that stuff. Things that can't be explained by science," she said, before giving him a pointed look. "Mermen."

"We prefer Merr." Iason didn't look offended by her words though.

"Merr," she repeated, nodding. "I will be sure to keep that in mind."

"But you believe in science," he countered. His expression fell as he studied a berry intently. "You were on a boat of scientists, were you not?"

"How...?" Cassandra stopped on her way to grab a berry and sat back. "I've been meaning to ask, but I wasn't sure how or when to say it. What happened to the others on my ship? Are they all right? Are they on this island?"

His fallen expression said it all, and he looked away from her. Silence filled the room as she took a deep breath and then another. Truth be told, she didn't know any of the others very well, but it was still sad. Finally, he said, "There was another from your ship. Bridget. She is here as well."

Bridget?

"Here?" Cassandra asked. "In this house?"

Iason smiled softly. "No, she is in the palace at Atlas."

"A palace? Wow," Cassandra said. "How did she score the palace?"

Iason frowned.

"It was a joke," Cassandra said. "I'm grateful to you for sharing your lovely home. It's beautiful."

He nodded once, as if to thank her for the compliment.

"So you have kings and queens and such?"

"Aye. We have a king. He has not taken a queen."

"And what are you? A soldier at the palace?"

"No, a hunter."

"Ah, that's right. Iason the Hunter."

He grinned, finally eating the berry that had captured his attention. He reached for another, slightly adjusting his legs as he continued to lounge. Her eyes drew down, hoping for a peek of his male pride. She didn't get one.

"And what do you hunt?" Cassandra reached for the wine pitcher he'd left and picked up an empty glass. Pouring, she set it in front of him.

He nodded, gratefully. "Thank you."

She helped herself to a glass and sat down. Sipping the wine, she waited for him to answer. The drink was good, very fruity, like the kind she'd tasted on his lips.

"I hunt scylla. They are a spirit of the water that attacks ships."

"Where do they come from?"

"The sea," he said, and she got the impression he didn't want to talk about it.

She ate several pieces of fish, thinking about

what he'd said. "So Ator...Altar...what did you call this island?"

"Ataran."

"Ataran," she repeated. "And where exactly is Ataran?"

"Beneath you," he said, laughing when she gave him a dirty look.

"Fine. Where are we?"

"In the ocean," Iason said. He sat up, taking his wine.

"Are you being difficult on purpose?" Cassandra challenged, setting her glass down and raising a brow. "Or is it because you need to keep the location secret? Could you give me a basic idea of where we are? Southern Hemisphere, perhaps?"

"No, I answered. We are in the ocean, below the surface."

Cassandra froze, waiting for the rest of the joke. It never came.

Please God, don't let him be crazy.

Supernatural on earth she could take, and on some level, a hidden island with other life forms hiding from humans made logical sense. Maybe she was more logical than she'd given herself credit for.

Iason sighed. "I might as well tell you the story of how this came to be, since you are here now. Long ago, Ataran was the center of the civilized world. We ruled over much of the land and were a vast empire. Back then we were known as the Atlantes."

"Atlantis?"

"It is pronounced Atlantes," he corrected.

"Atlantes," she said softly. Atlantes? As in Atlantes-Atlantis, the world beneath the ocean?

Don't panic, Cassie. Here him out. Oh, God, please don't let him be in some kind of strange merman cult.

She wasn't sure why, but some of the calm she'd been feeling, the carefree sensation clouding her brain, began to clear somewhat. It was as if she awoke from the world between dream and sleep coming to complete awareness. "We were blessed by the gods, more specifically the god, Poseidon. Our lands were prosperous, and we always conquered in battle." Iason paused.

Cassandra took the opportunity to cut in. "Poseidon? The Greek god who controlled the ocean, right?"

"Aye, the god of many races. He ruled the sea, and he is the one who brought Ataran up from the ocean for us to bless us."

Okay. Her lover was a merman. That she could

handle. She believed in aliens and supernatural crea-tures for the simple fact that it was vain to think humans were the only intelligent life the higher powers had made. But now she was supposed to believe in the lost city of Atlantis and the god Poseidon? And if there was a Poseidon, there must be a Zeus or a Thor or a Mars or whoever else it was that hung out in their togas on Mt. Olympus with him. She tried to remember the old, stop-motion movies she'd watched as a kid.

Cassandra's mind raced. She suddenly wished she had paid more attention in history class. Mythology wasn't her strongest area of expertise.

"Are you all right?" he asked, eyeing her. "Do you need to rest?"

"Mm-hm, I'm fine." Cassandra nodded weakly, taking a long drink of wine to hide her expression. She wished the liquor was stronger. A stiff shot of her grandmother's bourbon sounded really good about now. "Please, go on. You were saying your god brought Ataran up from the ocean."

"Yes. Then, one day, to punish us, Poseidon cast the island back down into the sea, taking us with it. We became Merr, and I became the man you see before you now."

Cassandra relaxed, seeming to finally understand. "Oh, so your ancestors were cursed by Poseidon and that's how your civilization started."

Okay, she could buy that. It made so much more sense. He was talking about folklore.

"No," Iason said, sighing heavily.

"No?" She tensed. What did he mean, no?

"No."

"That isn't how you civilization started?" Cassandra bit her lip. She glanced at the garden, wondering if she was going to have to make a run for it. Why did the one man she had such incredible sex with, have to turn out to be a lunatic? Her heart beat quickened, each thud a little harder than the last. Was this the beginning of a panic attack?

"No, it wasn't our ancestors this happened to. I was there." Iason looked so earnest, she knew he believed what he was saying.

"How long ago?" Cassandra shook, not sure she wanted to hear more. Couldn't they go back to not talking? This only proved she should have got to know him first and then seduced him.

"Many centuries," he said.

Cassandra didn't move. Centuries? Crazy hunter man was trying to tell her he was centuries old? "You have been born again? Reincarnation?"

"No, I have only been born once."

"Oh, okay then." Her hands shook. Were the ceilings moving a little? Closing in on her?

"Do not judge us for it," he pleaded softly. His eyes sparkled like emeralds, drawing her in. He was so handsome. What was he even doing with her? He could surely have his pick of so many women. Why her? "We have changed over the years. We have learned from our mistakes. We are not the same people we were back then."

And what was she doing with him? This was something she should never have started. She should have considered her actions first. Had she taken too many pain pills? Did it cloud her judgment? This wouldn't be the first time they'd made her a little loopy.

"Before we were cast down, we had power," he continued, obviously with no clue of her skeptical, racing thoughts. "I am sure you know that the kingdom of the dead is a grim place. Can you blame us for not wanting to go there? We began to think we were immortal, or at least hoped we were. It turned out we were merely foolish. We stopped worshiping Poseidon and began to worship ourselves as gods on Earth."

"Uh-huh," Cassandra said lightly, nodding her

head. She tried her best to keep the patronizing tone out of her voice.

"We became lazy, taking all we'd been given for granted. When we had conquered everything and there were no more battles to fight, we raided our neighbors and took more than we needed to survive and we over cultivated our own lands. Then, one day, King Lucius, after much feasting and drinking to celebrate how great a people we were, proclaimed that he would never die, for he never wished to leave our beautiful country—land that was more exquisite than even the kingdom of the gods."

Cassandra set her glass down, ready to bolt. She nodded as he paused in his story. Just as soon as he looked away, she could make a run for it.

"You must not think ill of King Lucius. He only said what we were all thinking at the time and had said many times ourselves. But, that night was different. Poseidon watched the feasting and heard him. The god had finally had enough of our insolence. After that, he cursed us for our vanity and self-love and gave us what we thought we wanted—immortality and this land, our land. He condemned us to forever walk on our earthly paradise and nowhere else. He sent forth the floods that very same evening and plunged Ataran into the water, trapping us so we could never set foot on mortal soil again. Here we have remained on the bottom of the ocean, drifting aimlessly with the currents in what you know as Deep Ocean, the Abyss."

Okay. Time to run.

Cassandra leaped for the dining room door with surprising agility. She didn't know where she was going, only that it was time to go. She made it as far as the front door before Iason caught her about the waist.

Kicking and screaming, she hollered, "Let me go! Let go!"

"What is it?" He sounded worried. "Are you upset at what we did? Please, it was a long time ago. You know how vengeful the gods can be. We have atoned since then. We have changed. Please, believe me, Cassandra. You have no reason to fear the gods' wrath."

Cassandra stopped struggling. His grip loosened, and she pushed his hands from her waist. "For your information, I do not know how the gods could be. No one has believed in them for centuries. They are myths from Ancient Greece and Rome. Hollywood makes movies and children's cartoons about them for our entertainment."

"Cartoons?"

"Never mind, it's not important. My point is your gods don't exist anymore, Iason."

Iason paled. "I had hoped that misunderstanding had changed. Aidan said as much after we brought him down. He said the gods were myths. How can this be? I have seen them. I have felt their wrath raining down upon my head. They exist."

"That's another thing, Iason. Look outside. This is not the ocean. This is air we breathe and that is land. There is sunlight and darkness and trees. There aren't fish and water, and if there was an island underwater, surely someone would have found it by now, what with all our modern technology." Cassandra edged toward the door, wondering if she could distract him long enough to get free. But then what? She knew what was out there. Just lots and lots of trees.

"You can believe in the Merr, but you have doubts about the gods? There is a problem with your logic. You say you would have found us beneath the waves with all you have accomplished on the surface. Wouldn't the same be truer with an island above the waves? Wouldn't you have found that first?" He studied her intently, as if he could will her to understand and believe whatever he said because he said it. "We are in Deep Ocean, the Abyss. Your boats have not come this far down. Most humans do not survive the dive to Ataran. And if the gods did not want you to see it, you would not."

"We speak the same language," she said. "That long ago you would have spoken something else, not English."

"All here can understand each other. We cannot explain it," he answered.

Iason was so handsome, so earnest, and her body remembered all too eagerly how he'd touched her. Cassandra looked at him and then the door. What should she do? Her mind was scared. Her body wanted to stay. Her heart wasn't sure. All she knew was that her mind was clearing, and she wanted to believe him. Maybe they were both crazy.

"You want me to believe you carried me underwater to a secret island?"

"Aye." He nodded.

Cassandra bit her lip. "And the air we are breathing?"

"We are protected down here," he said.

"By the gods," she whispered, already knowing the rest of his answer before he said it. That was the hardest thing about arguing religion. If a person had faith, anything could be explained.

"Aye, by the will of the gods." Iason moved as if

to touch her but then pulled back. "I promise you, we have changed as a people. You do not have to fear our past transgressions. They are not yours."

"This is all just a little hard to believe, Iason, that's all. I'm sure you have changed," Cassandra said, only a little patronizing. She patted his arm but didn't touch him otherwise.

"But, you accepted the supernatural with ease, why not this?"

Cassandra couldn't answer him. He did have a point. Why could she accept one thing and not the other? Maybe she was in shock and hadn't realized it. Maybe it was because what she thought was a simple new species of merfolk was really a bunch of new things—new people, new gods, new world.

"There is more I should tell you about," he said.

Cassandra felt the beginnings of a migraine. She closed her eyes and shook her head. "No, not right now, Iason. Please, I'm not feeling very well and need to lie down. I'm suddenly very tired. I guess this has been more to deal with than I first thought."

She made a move to go toward the bedroom. When he tried to follow, she held up her hand and said, "No, not right now. I need to lie down alone."

"But..."

"No," she said sternly, shutting the door behind

her. She sank down on the floor, her back against the wood. Cassandra could almost feel him on the other side. Then, she heard his soft footfall walking away. She reached for a lock, but there was none.

Seeing the vase, she hauled it in front of the door. It was heavy and should hold. Though, as strong as Iason was, she doubted it would keep him out for long. It had gotten darker in the room. There were no windows, but she could only guess it was evening. Crawling into bed, she closed her eyes. The darkness eased her headache somewhat and soon she was fast asleep, dreaming of crazy merman hunters in under-water worlds.

IASON STARED AT THE DOOR. Maybe he'd said too much. It was just that when she'd accepted what he was, he had assumed she would be all right with who he was and where they were. Apparently, he had assumed wrong. The look on her face tore at him. It was as if she thought he'd gone mad.

Iason waited outside the bedroom door for a long time, waiting to see if she would come back out or invite him in. She didn't, and he didn't dare disturb her. If she was still sick, he didn't want to bother her or force her to talk to him. Turning his back on the bedroom door, he walked away.

Maybe it was best not to tell her the rest just yet. After all, there was time. In Ataran, the one thing they had plenty of, was time.

Going to the dining room, he sighed, picking up the tray. He knew she was hungry, but she'd barely touched the food since he'd walked in. If he had known she would be embarrassed, he would have waited longer before coming back. At least then she would have eaten more.

Iason was surprised at how much she'd healed in such a short time. When he'd connected to her, he'd felt the depth of her pain, still felt it, but he didn't wish to let on. How could he complain about the ache in his bones when she'd suffered through much worse? Glancing at the bedroom door as he passed to the kitchen, he sighed. Soon she wouldn't have to worry about the pain anymore.

CHAPTER 15

CASSANDRA DIDN'T KNOW how long she'd slept, but when she woke up the room was brighter and her headache was gone. She yawned, glancing around the empty room. The vase was moved back where it belonged, but the door was still closed. Seeing it, she needlessly looked around again. The room was still empty.

Cassandra sighed. Clothes were laid out at the end of the bed. They were different than the tunica she had put on the day before. She slid out of the blue material and leaned to pick up the dress. Seeing her stomach, she froze. It had filled out a little more. All from a couple of pieces of fish and some fruit? That didn't make sense. She ran her hands over her ribs. They didn't stick out as much. How was she gaining weight? It shouldn't have been possible, and yet she didn't feel bloated or sick.

It took her a second to figure the new style of gown out, but finally she got the square piece of material draped over her body in such a way that it covered all of her. The green material had thin gold threads woven into it to create a beautiful, almost glossy sheen, as the light hit it. Though it was thick, it was lightweight.

Cassandra shook her head as she again felt her stomach. There was too much going on right now for her to worry about a little weight gain. For one thing, she had Iason to consider. He was handsome, with the body of a god, and the 'weapon' of a conquering warrior. She shivered with longing. Gods knew she wanted to be conquered by him again.

Gods? Just great, his craziness was rubbing off on her.

That orgasm he'd given her had been intense— better than her best vibrator had ever done. Just thinking about it made her sex dampen with longing. Her nipples tingled, and she had the strongest urge to seek Iason out and jump his bones.

But, there was the tiny problem of his believing they lived underwater and that he was centuries old. It was just a little too farfetched to be believed lightly. Accepting that mermen could live longer than regular humans, did it stand to reason they were immortal, and that he had personally been punished by the god Poseidon?

If she believed that, then what did she do to piss Poseidon off to get sent down here? And why did the gods not show themselves to mortals anymore? Weren't they angry that no one believed in them except a bunch of crazy underwater merfolk?

Cassandra's head spun. It was too much to think about. Going to the door, she peeked out. The atrium was empty.

Stepping out of the door, her foot hit a tray. She looked down. Iason had left her food—slices of the large pink fruit and the little blueberries. There was also an assortment of nuts.

Crazy or not, the man was thoughtful.

Cassandra bent over and took a piece of fruit. Juice dribbled down her chin, but she didn't care. She was famished. Before she knew it, she was sitting on the floor, moaning in pleasure and stuffing her face. By the time she'd plowed through the whole tray, she was smiling happily and feeling better than she had in a long time.

Thankfully, Iason wasn't around to witness her little chow-fest. Her grandmother would roll over in her grave to know she was eating like a heathen. If anything, the woman had been a lady with manners.

Licking her fingers, she sighed. Cassandra really missed her grandmother. The woman was more of a parent to her than her mother and father had been. It wasn't that her parents didn't love her, they did. They had just been too busy for their daughter. Oddly, them not being around felt normal. She knew most people wouldn't understand that, but it was the way it was. When she'd been diagnosed, they'd wanted her to come home—to a house fully staffed with nurses.

A tear slipped over her cheek. Cassandra had cried so much, she was tired of it. Life certainly wasn't fair. It was all just a big illusion. Thinking of Iason, she sighed. So his illusion was a little stranger than most. If he was happy with it and he treated her well, who was she to protest it or condemn his ways? And, if it was real to him, who was she to say it wasn't real at all? Truth was usually just a matter of perception.

"I'm tired of thinking," she said to herself, bumping the back of her head against the wall in frustration. Then, rubbing her sore skull, she whined, "Ow. That was just stupid."

It was time to find Iason. Whatever he told her,

she would just nod and go with it. Why not be happy in her last days? Why not let him build her an illusion? He was a merman after all. If she could accept that, she could accept anything. So long as he didn't fall in love, nothing else mattered. She would not do that to him only to leave him. Her heart, well, that was another matter. Regardless of what happened, she would never burden him with it. And, when she felt her time was close, she would break it off and walk away—perhaps back into the ocean. There was poetry in that idea.

Standing, Cassandra picked up the tray and moved in the direction she'd seen him turn toward to get the wine the night before.

"It's a plan," she said under her breath.

Even so, her heart tightened at the idea of leaving him to go into the ocean to die. What was wrong with her? She couldn't care for a man she'd just met. So what that he saved her and treated her with kindness. Oh, and lest she forgets, that orgasm. She wasn't in love. It was pure, animalistic, throw-me-down and tie-me-up lust.

Cassandra shivered. Iason was bold. What would it be like to give in to every one of their fantasies together? What better memories to create, or pleasure to be had?

Her decision made, she walked into the kitchen. It was neat and tidy. Pots and pans hung along the wall. There was a water basin with a low faucet and hand pump, a fire pit in the middle of an island and a wooden baker's table with a jar of dark flour. Cassandra set the tray on the counter. Seeing a latch on the floor, she pulled it up. Cool air drifted up a dark stone stairwell. His refrigerator maybe?

"Hello?" There was no answer. Cassandra shut the latch. Looking around the kitchen, she called louder, "Iason?"

Receiving no answer, she wondered back to the atrium. After exploring the gardens and the dining room, she frowned. The house seemed lonely without him—so big and cold.

Cassandra went outside. The sky was darker than usual and the air was crisp. It looked like it might rain later. She drew her arms into her draping gown and hugged them to her naked waist. "Iason? Are you out here?"

Making her way down the stone steps, she walked along the front of the house. The place was huge, like a Roman temple. Her sandals swished against the grass, the thin blades cool against her toes.

"Iason? Are you out here?"

Still no answer.

Cassandra scanned the surrounding forest, feeling as if she were being watched. The little hairs on the back of her neck stood at attention, but she couldn't make out anything beyond the trees. Then, hearing a splash as she rounded the side of the house, she stopped. She saw the edge of a pond surrounded by trees. Another splash sounded, followed by slow clapping. Curious, she made her way to the back of the house. Iason stood by the water beneath a marble gazebo.

He clapped once and a round ball flew from the water at him. He caught it, bending over slightly. The breeze ruffled his short toga, letting her get a peek of a taut butt cheek. Cassandra bit her lip.

Damn, the man was gorgeous.

His blond hair swept around his head. A dark red cloak lay on the marble slab, discarded at his feet. She hugged her arms closer to her body, keeping quiet. She watched his toga for another peek. A breeze hit as he leaned over to toss the ball at the water. This time she was afforded a view of both bronzed cheeks.

Cassandra suppressed a moan. Obviously, the Merr didn't believe in underwear.

Well, bless his gods for that one.

She smiled, drawn to go to him. He clapped and

caught the ball, only to toss it overhand toward the water. Muscles rippled over his bare arm and shoulder.

Cassandra wanted to touch him. He was so firm, filled with such solid muscle. When he touched her she felt all soft and feminine. She felt protected. Going closer, she wanted to feel protected again.

CHAPTER 16

Iason heard Cassandra coming toward him. He'd caught his name on the wind but didn't turn to answer her. He wasn't sure what he would say. It was very clear she thought he was crazy.

Throwing the ball at his pet fish, Iason watched the ugly creature dive after it. The wind blew up his toga, and he heard her gasp. A smile curled his lips. Before he told her of their curse, she'd been staring at him like she wanted to jump over the table and devour him. The feeling was mutual, and he'd been up most of the night with a serious affliction just thinking about it. Knowing that they needed to talk first, had kept him from hopping over the table and eating his meal off her naked chest.

If she was attracted to him, it was a start. Iason had no problem succumbing to her desires for they were his desires as well. Bending over, he let the wind lift his toga more fully as he tossed the ball. As he listened to her footsteps, he detected her tripping feet, and his grin widened.

Cassandra obviously didn't know about the Merrs' sensitive hearing. He might not tell her just yet. It was adorable the way she would get tripped up and nervous around him. Her breathing often caught and changed with little provocation.

Iason clapped, caught the ball, and threw it back at the water. As his pet fish dove after it, she called, "Iason?"

Iason turned, glancing at her. He smiled. Her red hair blew exotically around her face, trailing along the wind. She was so pale, so delicate, that he wanted to wrap her in his arms and protect her always. Her arms were pulled inside her gown. Then, seeing how she'd wrapped the gown around her body, he chuckled. It was all wrong.

Cassandra stopped at his laugh, glancing down her body. "What?"

"The gown," he said. Iason let his eyes drift over her as he dipped his voice into a low, sultry tone. "Would you like me to show you how to drape it?"

Cassandra opened her mouth to speak but was stopped when his pet fish hit the ball back at him. It struck him in the side of the head with a loud thud. He blinked in surprise, turning to glare at the ugly little animal. The creature swam back and forth, mocking him.

Cassandra laughed. It was a beautiful sound. Iason rubbed the side of his head, giving her a playfully grumpy look. She joined him on the platform.

To his pleasure, she pulled her arms from the gown and reached up to touch his temple lightly where the ball had hit. Then, leaning over, she picked the ball up and eyed the pond. "What are you doing?"

Iason clapped. The ugly little fish surfaced, wagging his tail fins.

"Please don't tell me that's Poseidon," she said dryly, arching a brow.

Iason laughed. "No."

"Your wife?" she asked, eyeing him strangely.

Iason jerked, repulsed by the very idea. "Gods no! We do not mate with fish."

Her lips curled up ever so slightly, and he realized she was goading him.

"This is my pet. He kept following me around in the ocean when I hunted. Finally, it got to the point where he would never leave the Crystal Caves at Atlas, where we go out into the Abyss. When the others would try to hunt, he would nip at their tail-fins. So, I brought him here. He rules this whole lake and seems content enough.

"What's his name?"

"I call him Ugly," Iason admitted. He looked at his pet, as if seeing it for the first time. It was hideous. The others had teased him mercilessly about his new 'woman-friend'. Ugly had teeth as sharp as razors, a huge head and a smaller spiny tail. Its eyes were a milky blue, and it was a wonder the creature could see the ball he tossed at him.

Cassandra motioned as if she would toss the ball. He nodded for her to go ahead. She gave it a light toss. The fish looked at the ball as it sank, then at her. It didn't move. Cassandra frowned slightly, a hurt look in her eyes. "It doesn't like me."

"Ugly," Iason barked, scolding the fish. The creature looked at him and it was almost as if he could see the pout on its vicious mouth. It dove underwater. "Ah, ignore him. He's pouting."

"Pouting?" Cassandra smirked. "About what?"

"He's jealous that you are up here with me during his play time. I do not make it out to the country too often." Iason stepped closer to her, watching to see if she would back away. She didn't.

"Why's that? It's beautiful out here." Cassandra looked at his mouth, and he licked his bottom lip, liking the way she shivered in reaction.

"To reach the ocean we must be in Atlas at the palace. I have a home there as well. It is where I stay most of the time," he said.

Cassandra gasped, her eyes widening. "You live at the palace? Are you a prince?"

Iason took his finger and pushed at her jaw, shutting her slack mouth. "No. I am a hunter. Hunters are an honored position. We bring things back from the surface world."

"Like women?"

"Aye, though mostly we hunt the scylla and locate mortal artifacts so that the scavengers may go and retrieve them."

"You mean sunken ships, don't you?"

"Aye."

"And since you hunt the scylla and they sink ships, you generally know where to send the scavengers to look." Cassandra took a deep breath and held it.

"Aye." Iason nodded sadly. "But we do not let them sink the ship if it can be helped."

Cassandra nodded. "You didn't have to explain. I know that."

He smiled, her words bringing him pleasure. Maybe she'd just been in shock. Hearing that she was in a new world had to be a hard thing for her to process as a mortal. If he just gave her a little time, surely she would come around.

"So," she said, turning to the water. "Exactly how many women have you brought back?"

His smile turned into a full grin. "Jealous?"

"No," she answered, a little too loud.

"Really." He shrugged. "Then why ask?"

"Ah!" Cassandra hit his arm. He laughed at her feeble punch. There was no way she could do him any harm with her small fists. But, to be fair, he did lean away from her, affecting a scared look. Grumbling, she waved her hand in dismissal and gave up. "Ah, quit patronizing me. You are so big I would need a submarine to knock you over."

"You think I'm big?" he asked, his words holding a double meaning. She instantly blushed.

"Strong," she squeaked, her blush deepening until her cheeks were bright red. "I meant strong."

He took an aggressive step closer. "So, you don't think I'm big?"

Her round eyes glanced down his body, straying

on his lower stomach. Iason was already aroused from the night spent thinking about her. It did not take long for his cock to catch up. The blood flowed in a rush down to his member, lifting the toga. Cassandra gasped.

"Very," she whispered, breathlessly.

"You think I'm very big?" he teased.

She looked up at him, instantly denying, "I didn't say that."

"Mm," he hummed softly. Lifting a finger to her oddly draped gown, he offered, "I can show you..."

Cassandra's breath caught when he purposefully paused, and she again glanced down his body. Her little pink tongue darted out over her bowed lips. It was glorious torture.

"...how to drape this gown, if you like," he finished.

She blinked, and he thought it adorable the way she was caught off guard by him. Her mouth opened, but no sound came out. He drew his finger down her shoulder to skim the side of her breast. Long lashes fluttered over her eyes.

Iason leaned in to steal a kiss. Just then, Ugly hit the ball with his tail, sending it flying. It knocked Iason hard in the temple only to bounce off his head to lightly graze Cassandra's ear. They both turned to the water to see Ugly swimming around.

Cassandra giggled. "I definitely think he does not like me."

Seeing her shiver from the cool breeze, he reached for his cloak and slipped it over her shoulders. "Let's get you in from the cold, shall we?"

As he led her toward the house, he turned to glare at Ugly. The fish only seemed to glare back before diving under the pond's murky surface. Iason pressed his hand lightly to Cassandra's back, guiding her to the front of the house.

"You said you have caretakers?" she asked. "Where are they?"

"I received word about a week ago that they went to visit friends," he answered.

"How does that work?" Cassandra glanced at him. "I mean, do you pay them? Are they servants?"

"Aye. We have an arrangement. They look after my property, live here, eat my food, do as they will, so long as the estate is maintained, and when I come home we coexist peacefully."

"And if they were to have children?" Cassandra asked. "Would they live here too?"

Iason's gut tightened. He could not look at her.

Dropping his hand from her back, he said quietly, "The Merr do not have children."

"Do not or cannot?"

"Do not," he answered, not wanting to talk about it. "And most likely cannot."

"Oh," she touched his arm, threading her chilled fingers over it. "I'm sorry."

"It is the way of things," he said.

They walked around the front of the house in silence. Iason automatically opened the door for her. She smiled shyly at him before walking inside. Glancing down over her figure, he would swear she had filled out a little—her slencer waist leading into the gentle slope of her hips and ass.

"Thank you for leaving me the tray for breakfast this morning," she said once he'd closed the door.

Iason nodded, not hearing the words as he continued to look her over. Cassandra blushed, her cheeks turned pink. He wondered if her blush traveled all the way to her breasts, matching the shade of her pink nipples.

By all the gods! He wanted to make love to her.

Iason took an aggressive step forward. She bit at her lip only to lick at it with her tongue. His cock was so hard for her. He could practically feel her body on his, her tight wet passage. Licking his lips, he wondered if she would let him drink from her again.

"We should talk more," she said, her chest rising and falling with each heavy breath. "Yesterday, you said there was more to your story. What more?"

"Aye, there is more." Iason barely paid attention to his words as he answered her. He was too busy thinking of positions he would like to take her in. With the pleasure nymph over the many long years, he'd been able to get creative. Right now, he just looked back at that as training to pleasure the woman before him.

"Tell me," she insisted.

Why was she backing away? Still not heeding his words, he said, "Because I brought you here, you will turn into one of us. You will be Merr."

Cassandra gasped. Iason's eyes darted up, instantly aware of what he'd said a second after it was out. She bit her lip. "You are going to make me into a mermaid?"

"The gods will." Did they have to discuss this now? He wanted her so badly. It was all he could do not to rip off her clothes and pin her against the marble wall. She was so light, Iason was sure he could manage the position easily.

"And you think I will become immortal?"

"Aye."

Cassandra took a deep breath. Then, to his great surprise, she said, "Okay."

"You are fine with this?" he asked.

"Sure." Her tone was unconvincing. He could see the doubt in her eyes as she tried to hide it from him. Didn't she believe him? "Why not, right?"

"I'm telling you the truth," he insisted.

"Okay."

"You will become Merr." He frowned. She really didn't believe him.

"Whatever you say," she answered. When he stopped moving toward her, she came toward him. Her hand skimmed lightly over the side of her breast before trailing over her hip, tempting him to reach forward and touch her the same way. He was torn between the need to make her believe and the need to make love to her.

"Cassandra—?"

"I'm hungry, Iason." Her bottom lip pouted out. "Would you take some food to the dining room for me?"

His throat tight, he asked, "What would you like?"

"Some of that fruit," she answered. "Please."

How could he deny that look anything? Iason

nodded, watching her turn and walk through the gardens. Practically stumbling over his feet, he ran to the kitchen. He grabbed a knife, cutting into the fruit. In his haste the slices were all uneven. Not caring, he grabbed a platter, forgot the serving tray, and ran toward the dining hall. Stopping before she could see him, he began to walk.

CHAPTER 17

CASSANDRA TOOK A DEEP BREATH, lounging on the dining room pillow-chair. A mermaid? She tried not to laugh. His innocent superstitions were kind of cute. Well, if he wanted to believe she would turn into a fish-woman, so be it. What harm was there in indulging him? Besides, she liked the fantasy of it.

Her body was on fire for him, and, as far as she saw it, she still owed him a little return favor from the day before. Her mouth watered thinking of the fruit. This was going to be so much fun.

Pulling on her gown, she made it dip lower in the front before pulling the material tight against her nipples. She pinched them, making them hard. Little jolts of pleasure worked through her as she touched herself. She'd taken off his cloak, letting it lay over the pillow.

Iason appeared, carrying a tray. He walked fast, and she smiled knowing he was eager to be with her. She lounged back as he came into the dining room. His beautiful eyes instantly went to her breasts. Staring at them he set the tray down on the table.

"Join me?" she asked, pretending not to notice as she grabbed a piece of fruit.

He kicked off his sandals and lounged across from her. Cassandra sat up, sucking the fruit slice slowly between her lips. She absently kicked off her shoes, moaning at the delicious pleasure as she swallowed the juice.

Iason stared at her mouth. Cassandra took a bite and chewed slowly. "Mm, delicious. What do you call this?"

"Auv," he answered

"Mm, auv." Cassandra took a fresh piece and stood. A little sugary sweet stream ran down her wrist, and she licked it slowly, keeping her eyes on him as she did so. Iason's whole body tensed. He did not move.

Cassandra came around to his lounge pillow. Stepping beside him, she ate the small slice. Then, taking her fingers, she ran it along his thigh. Starting at the knee, she pushed up, gently lifting his toga higher. His muscles tensed. She stopped on his hip, not exposing his erection. With a gentle push, she urged him to roll on his back. He obeyed.

Cassandra ran her hand back down, pushing his thighs apart so the foot closest to her fell on the floor. Then, sitting where his leg had been, she reached across the table for more fruit. She leaned over him, rubbing the piece on his bottom lip. "Try it."

He bit into it, sucking the piece between his lips. Iason didn't take his eyes off her. When he reached out to touch her, she batted his hand away.

"Don't. I'm eating right now." Cassandra smiled playfully at him, batting her eyelashes as she demanded, "It is good, isn't it?"

He eagerly nodded, chewing slowly. She reached for another piece, taking the biggest slice. Purposefully, she let the fruit juice drip on his inner thigh. It made slow trails over his flesh, slipping down onto the cushion beneath him.

"Oops. Look at the mess I'm making." Shaking her head, she forced a sigh. His eyes widened. He stopped chewing, staring at the drops and then her.

Cassandra pushed his other leg over the side. The toga still covered his arousal. Leaning over, she licked his thigh. Iason groaned, closing his eyes.

"Mm, delicious," she said. When he again looked at her, she licked her lips. Squeezing the fruit, she dribbled juice on his other leg. Affecting a pout, she said, "Oh, dear. Look how clumsy I'm being today."

Iason's lids fell heavily over his eyes and his mouth opened as if waiting for what was to come. Cassandra licked his thigh clean. He smelled good— like fresh air and soap. When she'd licked it all up, she took the hand with the slice in it and drew the fruit up his thigh. Her mouth never left him as she licked up after the trail. Her hand reached under his tunic, pushing it up to expose his delicious body as she made a sugary sweet path up his hip. Flicking her tongue over his sexy lower stomach, she moaned softly before pulling back.

"I should eat this before I make more of a mess." Cassandra bit into the fruit, letting the juice dribble down onto his towering erection. Glancing down, she pushed out her lip and gave him a playfully apologetic look. "Oops."

"You will kiss me there?" he asked, sounding awed. His large shaft strained up from his hips. The juice trail had hit his tip, running over the side.

She smiled. It did stand to reason if the Merr didn't practice oral sex male on female, then they probably didn't do female on male. This was going to be better than she thought.

"I'm just cleaning up after myself." Cassandra squeezed the fruit, drizzling his shaft with it. She smiled, not even pretending it was an accident. He looked as if he would reach out to her but then threaded his hands behind his head. His stomach tensed and jerked with each drip of fruit juice. When his erection was thoroughly coated, she tossed the crushed fruit slice back on the plate.

Leaning over, she licked the tip of his shaft, rimming the little hole. She flicked her tongue over the mushroomed head, moaning softly with each lick, telling him how good the fruit tasted on him. "Mm. Delicious."

Cassandra let the tip of her tongue follow the veins along the side. She took her time, torturing and pleasuring him. He groaned, grunting and panting incoherently for more, as she licked his shaft from root to tip. His gorgeous body strained. The rigid muscles of his defined stomach were so tight.

She had to open her mouth wide to fit him in. Sucking his tip between her teeth, she dipped her mouth over him as far as she could go. His body spasmed and his hips bucked up, nearly choking her with his girth. Needing both hands to finish the task, she gripped the root of his penis and twisted her fingers over the thick shaft.

Cassandra sucked him, working her hands and mouth eagerly on his shaft. The taste of him mixed with the fruit was exotic and addictive. Iason groaned, arching his back. A shiver went over his entire length. His muscles strained beautifully and he came with a loud groan, releasing his seed down her throat.

When she pulled back, a satisfied smile on her face, she met his fiery gaze. With lightning speed, he flung her on her back. "My turn."

Cassandra tried to touch him, but he captured her wrists and pinned them over her head. With a tug, he ripped through the material covering her breasts. It was her turn to be tortured.

Iason squeezed the juice on her nipples, sucking and nipping at her breasts until they were clean. Then, releasing her wrists, he drizzled her thighs with juice, pushing the gown up to expose her legs. Cassandra moaned. She'd never felt anything so highly erotic. He took it slowly. By the time she finally felt him latch onto her sex she was ready to scream in frustration.

Iason pleasured her with an eager force. She'd never heard of a man who liked going down as much as this one obviously did. His mouth suctioned to her and he twirled her clit with his tongue. She was in such a heightened state of arousal, that she came almost immediately.

Pleasure ripped through Cassandra, causing her to moan and scream at the same time. He gentled his movements, but kept going, milking her body for all it had. When she could give him no more, he stopped and grinned wickedly up from between her thighs. "Mm, delicious."

CHAPTER 18

OVER THE NEXT SEVERAL DAYS, they made love in a variety of places and ways. Cassandra was happy, content to be with him, as she lost track of all time. It could have been a week or a month. She didn't care. It was as if they had created a world where nothing else mattered, where she didn't have to think about tomorrow.

Iason was kind, treating her like a princess. He gave her beautiful gowns to wear and he insisted on cooking for her. More often than not, he also insisted on feeding his creations to her by hand. They talked of many things, of themselves, of their worlds. They never once discussed the future and if Iason even tried, she would kiss him until he forgot all about it.

MICHELLE M. PILLOW

Then, one day, it started to rain. The atrium pool had been too hard to resist and they made love in it. The rain pelted them from above as he lifted her up onto his body. It was terribly romantic—their flesh gliding with cool rainwater, their bodies joining as he held her up, his muscles bulging sexily. Afterward, Iason carried her to the bed and they slept in each other's arms. When she awoke, he was toying with her damp hair, staring at her.

"You are getting better," Iason said softly. "Your color is good with a flush to your cheeks. We should make the journey to the palace."

Cassandra sighed. "I like it here. It's so beautiful —the trees, the dark sky, Ugly. I don't want to leave."

"We don't even leave the house," he teased. Then, quirking a brow, he asked, "And you think Ugly is beautiful?"

She giggled. "Okay, well maybe not him, but the pond is, and Ugly does have a charm all his own. Plus, I think he is taking to me. Last time when he tossed the ball at my head, it wasn't as hard."

Iason chuckled. "He'll come around. How can he resist you?"

His eyes seemed to say, 'how can anyone resist you?'

She smiled, doing her best to hide the blush that tried to cross over her features.

"We must go to the palace," Iason said. "Many will want word that you are all right."

Cassandra pushed up on the mattress to study him. "Do you have to go back to work? I mean, hunting."

"Aye, I will in time," he said. "But not right away. I saved you, and I must take care of you." When her expression began to falter, he quickly added, "A duty that is not burdensome whatsoever, I assure you."

"Then, why must we go?" She frowned, confused. "Why not stay here? Can't we just send word that I'm alive, well, and wish to reside in the country for a while?"

Iason touched her face. "We go to the palace so you can announce to the king that you wish to marry me."

Cassandra stared at him. If he would have sprouted horns and turned green she would have been less shocked. Was he proposing to her?

She sat up, looking around the bedroom. Her heart beat really fast and hard. He couldn't be doing this to her. How did she let things progress this far? The plan was to love him and leave him. That's it. He was not supposed to fall in love with her.

"Cassandra?" he asked, touching her back. Unable to help herself, she jolted at the contact.

"I have to use the bathroom." She stood and pulled a tunica over her head. "I'll be right back. Keep the bed warm for me."

He smiled, but his eyes were confused. She took one last glance before closing the door behind her. His handsome face stayed with her.

Cassandra took a deep breath. She had a plan, and she was going to keep it. He wanted to marry her so it was time to go. Never mind that she was happy with him, that she had somehow fallen madly in love with him.

She went to the front door and slipped out into the cool weather. The rain had stopped, but the ground was still soggy. Iason's bedroom didn't have any windows, so he wouldn't be able to see her run for the trees. Tears streamed down her face and her feet slipped in the mud, but she pushed on.

It's not fair! It's not fair! Why?

There was a terrible ache inside her chest and it only got worse with each beat of her heart. Why give her all this happiness only to take it away? She'd been ready to go before Iason. She'd made her peace with death. Now she'd met the handsome hunter and he was wonderful and funny and gorgeous and sexy and so many things that she'd never had before.

Cassandra ran faster, suppressing the urge to scream. She wanted to live, had never had so much to live for. The gods were cruel—all of them, his, hers. She hated them all.

Her days had been good, but the doctors had told her to expect that. She would have good and bad days, but in the end, her cancer was terminal. She stopped running, collapsing on the ground in a fit of crying. Cassandra took a deep breath and then another, trying to calm down. It wasn't fair. She'd finally found something wonderful, something worth keeping and it was going to be taken away from her.

"I love him," she whispered, silently begging whoever listened to let her have her life back. "Please, I love him. I do not want to lose him."

"Ah," a feminine voice answered, the tone mocking. Cassandra shivered, looking up. A beautiful woman stood before her in a skimpy translucent gown, revealing her naked body in all its perfection. "How touching. She loves him."

"Are...?" Cassandra shivered, wiping her eyes.

"She doesn't want to lose him," another female answered. "She loves him."

The woman tilted her head to the side. Her long black hair fluttered in the breeze. She was beautiful, perhaps the most beautiful woman Cassandra had ever seen.

"Are you a goddess?" Cassandra managed after staring for some time. Had the gods come down to answer her plea? Was Iason right? Did all the gods on Mt Olympus come down to walk amongst them? Were her prayers going to be answered?

"I am Queen Maia," the woman answered, obviously amused by the question. She reached leisurely, almost lovingly, toward Cassandra's cheek before tipping her head back and laughing. Soon other voices joined hers. Cassandra couldn't see the others, only the queen. "And you, my dear, are my newest pet."

Glancing around the trees, she watched as a redheaded woman with matching red eyes stepped from the forest. She too wore a translucent robe. It fluttered in the breeze. When she walked, her bare feet didn't make a sound.

There was a cruelness apparent in the redhead, and she suddenly saw it mimicked in the eyes of the queen. Maia's gaze narrowed in spite as she studied her.

"Leave me alone," Cassandra said.

"Humans," the redhead spat, shivering in obvious disdain. "You dare to command us? You, a little mortal girl?"

"Patience, Lotis," Maia said, her tone dripping with sweetness. Lotis' red eyes glowed eerily. "You'll have your fun with her soon enough, as will we all."

"I cannot believe they brought her down and then lost her." Lotis sneered. "What is this forest coming to?"

Laughter again sounded and soon more beautiful women joined them, circling around Cassandra. Each wore a translucent robe and long hair flowed over their shoulders. They were in great shape, almost goddess-like in appearance. But there was nothing divine about the way the women eyed her, or the way their lips curled in cruel smiles.

Maia made a move to touch her. Cassandra darted to her feet and tried to run. A tall blonde stepped in her path, grabbing her arms with surprising strength.

"Leave me alone," Cassandra said. "Take your hands off me."

The woman laughed, a hard, nasty sound.

"What's your name, pet?" the blonde demanded.

Cassandra shook her head in denial, struggling to

get free. The blonde glanced behind Cassandra's back, not letting go. Maia appeared at their side.

"So be it," Maia sighed. "We will do it your way, pet."

Maia punched her in the face. Cassandra moaned, instantly passing out.

CHAPTER 19

IASON FROWNED, crawling out of bed. Something was wrong. He hadn't meant to upset Cassandra but had just assumed she knew they were married. When the gods sent her to him, and let her survive in the ocean, he'd accepted that the gods knew what they were doing. He'd been attracted to her from the beginning, perhaps had even loved her though he'd been hesitant to admit it. Why else would he risk everything to save her? And why else would she be so willing to come to him, to kiss him in that first moment beneath the ocean waves?

True, they never talked of love when they were together, not even in the most intimate of moments. Iason just assumed she knew how he felt and that it didn't need to be said with words. It was ordained by the gods, after all, even if she didn't exactly believe him about Poseidon.

How could Cassandra not know how he felt about her? It was all over his face, pouring out with each beat of his heart. He would swim to the ends of the ocean and back if she so commanded it. He would do anything for her.

When she was in his bed, making love to him, she didn't seem to mind his open adoration of her. Why then did saying the words out loud upset her? Every time he tried to talk about them, she would kiss him to silence. Maybe he should have resisted more and made her hear him out.

Merr were passionate people, and all of Iason's passion was for her. He wanted to spend the rest of his days making love to her, hunting the seas to make her proud to be the wife of a great and respected hunter. Already her desires matched his. Someday soon her body would change as she became a Merr woman. Insatiable passion was one of the first signs, and she definitely had that.

Cassandra had resisted the depths of euphoria, the state that most saved humans went through. Althea had warned him that because she'd been sick before he rescued her that she might be resistant due to the numbing found in her blood. Or, perhaps, the gods felt she didn't need to be as dazed as the others, because she accepted the Merr without fear, even if she did look skeptically at him from time to time when he said something—as if she couldn't quite bring herself to believe him. But, if she accepted as much as she did, accepted that his kind existed, why not something as simple as being his wife?

Grabbing a cloak, he draped it over his body and went to the bathroom door. He knocked lightly. "Cassandra?"

A sick feeling curled inside him. Somehow he felt that she wasn't in there. He opened the door, confirming his fears. He didn't need to check the rest of the house. Cassandra had left him. He said they were married, and she had run out on him.

His heart beat erratically in his chest. Iason hurried to the front door, instantly seeing her muddy footprints leading toward the forest. Without stopping to get shoes, he ran after her. Why would she run from him, from them? Wasn't she happy? Didn't he give her everything she wanted? Didn't he take care of her? She said she liked the house, the food, even said she didn't want to go back to the palace so soon. She liked him. Her body screamed, '*yes*', but her actions now said, '*no*'.

"Cassandra!" he yelled, running faster. Surely

she couldn't get too far from him before he caught her. He was much stronger and used to strenuous physical activity. Suddenly, the tracks stopped. It was as if she'd paced in circles, making prints everywhere. Iason froze, seeing a shell necklace left on the ground. "Or others were here with her."

Iason glanced around, fear tightening in his gut. He couldn't feel anyone in the forest watching him. Scowling, he leaned over and picked up the shell necklace.

"Maia," he swore, using her name like a curse as he fingered the smooth shells.

The Olympians, as they called themselves after the gods of Mt. Olympus, did not want the humans brought to Ataran for they looked at the Merr curse as a blessing. Not to mention Maia had declared herself Queen of the Olympians after King Lucius refused to marry the spiteful mermaid. She and her followers believed themselves to be goddesses below the waves. Before the Crystal Caves were sealed, the Olympians had lured humans to their deaths for sick pleasure. They were the reason the caves were off limits except to those with permission. The Merr did not want the gods punishing the rest of them for the continued vanity of Maia and her Olympians.

A small faction of Maia's mad followers were said

to live in the forest, but it had been decades since they had shown themselves. Seeing the pendant on the necklace, carved into the shape of a dolphin, he knew that the deranged women had finally resurfaced. If they had Cassandra, then they would soon be thirsting to kill humans again. Bloodlust could be tempered but never cured.

Iason dropped the necklace back on the path. Scanning the forest, he began the long search for footprints that would show him the way. The Olympians were experts at covering their tracks but obviously wanted their presence to be known, for they had left the necklace for him to find. Were they taunting him?

"What are you up to, Maia?" he whispered. "Why show yourself now, after all these years? Why take my wife?"

CHAPTER 20

CASSANDRA MOANED WEAKLY. The ground shifted beneath her, causing her body to rock back and forth in an almost sickening rhythm. Opening her eyes, she focused on the forest floor as it edged further and further away from her. Screaming, she tried to push up on the planks beneath her, but the platform wobbled and she was forced back down as a foot pressed into the center of her back. Bare toes dug into her spine, twisting into her flesh.

"Quiet, mortal!" someone hissed in her ear. Cassandra felt a hand replacing the foot on her back as the woman leaned over her to speak. "Or we will kick you over the edge just to watch you splat."

Cassandra gripped a wood post as another woman nudged her ribs. She tried to get her bearings.

They were high off the ground, too high to jump. Then, turning her head to look up a pair of long legs, she saw a female guard holding a spear. The woman ignored her, but Cassandra couldn't help staring. She looked just as Cassandra would have pictured an Amazonian warrior to be. The guard was dressed in a fur-lined bikini top that barely covered her large breasts and a skimpy loincloth that showed off the bottom curve of her butt—at least from Cassandra's view on the platform.

Suddenly, the platform stopped half way up the cliff by a cave opening. The warrior woman who had caught Cassandra's notice finally turned to her only to snarl in disgust as she hauled the prisoner roughly to her feet.

Cassandra shivered to discover she was surrounded by even more women. Many wore the same transparent dresses of her captors, with bracelets that wound around their arms, and delicate shell necklaces around their necks. A couple wore headbands, woven around their long hair to keep it out of their face, and matching woven armbands.

The warrior guard, who had brought her to her feet, pushed her forward. She stumbled into a cave. The hole in the cliff opened up to a long area, covered in lounge pillows sewn from the canvas of ships. Fine, gauzy material fluttered over the rock walls, matching the translucent gowns of her captors.

"Welcome to Mt. Olympus, mortal." Maia bumped into her shoulder as she walked past into the cave. Cassandra grimaced. The queen turned to a woman with long brown hair who lounged next to a low waterfall. "Electra, show our new pet to her room. No mistakes this time. Lock her up."

Electra nodded once and stood gracefully, her body's movements reminiscent of a ballerina. Water dripped from an opening in the stone, trickling into a long pool that wound around the side of the cave. The mermaids in the pond floated on the surface, their tails swishing in the water. Everyone was watching her, their gazes unwelcoming. Electra moved away from the pond, walking across the large cave room to the other side. She didn't wait to see if the prisoner would follow.

Someone shoved Cassandra's back, and she fell forward. The mermaids laughed at her. Cassandra stood, proudly lifting her chin. She would not give them the satisfaction of seeing her fear.

When she didn't move to follow Electra, Maia ordered, "Junia, help Electra show our pet to her—no, wait."

Cassandra shivered at the evil pleasure on the queen's face as an idea dawned in her malicious eyes.

"Show our pet first to Lysander's room." Maia grinned. "Make her serve him."

"Serve a slave?" Someone asked.

Maia's smile only widened. Cruel laughter sounded over them. "Yes, Neda. She will serve a slave. Our new pet will be a slave's slave."

Cassandra tried to bolt, but the big Amazonian mermaid stepped in her way, knocking her back.

"Tell him not to show her kindness," Maia yelled.

Suddenly, hands were on Cassandra's body, and she was dragged deeper into the cave, kicking and cursing. The women pulled her down a long hall before stopping at a wooden door. It was locked.

"Open it," Electra ordered. The door was unlocked by another Amazonian guard, and Cassandra was thrust in. To her surprise, a man stood up from a lush bed. His solid body glistened with oil and he wore only a loincloth. Taking one look at Cassandra, he instantly kneeled, "My queen, I am Lysander. I am here for your pleasure."

Electra laughed, throwing back her head. "She is not one of your queens, slave. You are her king. Break her spirit."

"Yes, my queen," Lysander said, bowing his head

once more. Sculpted, tanned muscle rippled over his chest as he moved.

Cassandra glanced at the big man. He looked up into her eyes from his place on the ground, seeming to glare at her in devious pleasure. She ran to the door screaming.

"Lysander! Control her." Electra ordered.

Cassandra fought as Lysander grabbed her from behind, holding her close to his firm body.

"Mind your mortal," Electra ordered. "Gag her if you have to, but keep her quiet. Queen Maia will not wish to hear the slave pet's screams in her delicate royal ears."

Lysander wrapped a large palm over her mouth, his fingers digging into skin. Cassandra pleaded with the mermaids for help with her eyes as she struggled to be free. She watched the one, Neda, give her a small, pitying smile before turning her eyes to Lysander. She felt the man stiffen behind her, but Neda closed the door and locked them in.

"Will you be quiet so they have no cause to come back?" he demanded.

Cassandra nodded. He relaxed, letting her go. Cassandra pulled away from him, inching as far away as she could in the small room.

"What do you want with me?" Cassandra took a

MICHELLE M. PILLOW

deep breath, but she couldn't stop trembling. If this large man decided to attack and 'break her spirit', she would be unable to stop him.

"It is not what I want, it is what they want," he said. "It is always what they want. The sooner you accept it, the better it will be for you." He snorted in self-depreciating laughter. "Good luck to you if you can figure that one out. I don't think they even know what they want anymore. Sometimes I think they merely act out of boredom, because they don't know what to do with their endless days."

Cassandra looked him over. "You're a slave."

Lysander's face hardened, looking nothing like when he bowed to the mermaids. Harshly, he said, "So are you. Worse, even, they called you a pet."

"But, look at you. You're so big. Why not fight them? Why not run away? Surely you can take a bunch of women."

"And go where?" he asked.

"You're Merr. Go to Atlas. Go to your people."

"I've got news for you, baby doll. I'm mortal, same as you. I have no people here. And, besides, I have seen what Queen Maia is capable of when you try to escape her. I may be a big man, but don't underestimate those mermaids' strength. I can't take them all on."

"What?" Cassandra asked, eyeing him. "What does the queen do? Surely whatever punishment she comes up with isn't as bad as being her slave."

"You ever watch someone filet and gut a live fish?"

Cassandra read the meaning in his eyes and shivered. She covered her mouth, suddenly nauseous. "Oh."

"It is better to serve in paradise than to rot in the bottom of the ocean," he said bitterly.

Cassandra trembled at his dark look. "Are you going to rape me now?"

Lysander frowned, going to sit on the bed. "Only if you make me."

"I am in love with someone. I will not sleep with you willingly. I can't."

Lysander chuckled. "What's love got to do with anything around here, sweetheart? Don't you know the only thing these women put stock in is sex? The Olympians are very sexual creatures and get much of their power from sexual release. Believe me. It is not pretty when they don't get their fix. Queen Maia uses abstinence as a punishment for the disobedient mermaids. If they are really bad, we have to heat them up and deny them release."

Cassandra slumped against the wall, sensing

that he wasn't going to hurt her for the time being. Still, she kept a wary eye on him. "Where did you come from? How did you get here if you're not Merr?"

"I'm from the surface world, same as you. They brought me down here many years ago. Harlots pretended like they were drowning and lured me into the water. Next thing I know I wake up on this underwater paradise surrounded by naked woman. Fool that I was, I thought it was heaven, until they made me realize it was hell. Slaves have one purpose and one purpose only—to pleasure the queens in any way and time they see fit."

"They are all queens?" Cassandra frowned. She rubbed her temples, trying to make sense of what was happening. This morning she was with Iason, now she was held captive by a bunch of bloodthirsty, sex crazed mermaid queens.

"To us they are. To them, Maia is their queen. I suggest you start to address them as such. Maia likes to give lashes with her whip."

Cassandra nodded in understanding. She tried not to think of Iason. Somehow, part of her believed he would save her. "So you are not going to make me sleep with you?"

"Sleep, yes. Sex, not unless I have to," he said.

"When it's all I do all day, believe me talking to a woman becomes the real pleasure."

"How many slaves are here?"

"Dozens." Lysander lay on his back. "They pick us for our stamina and youth. Sometimes I think the lucky ones are the poor old souls they drown when fishing for us."

Cassandra felt sorry for the man, for all of the men the Olympians brought down. She stood, looking around the small room. There wasn't anything special about it. It was a wonder Lysander was even sane, being kept in such a prison for so many years.

"So, you are in love?"

"Yes." Cassandra nodded. "I am."

"It would be best for you to keep it from your mind. Forget him if you have to. You can't get back to him. Once you are down here there is no going back to the surface."

Cassandra shivered. "We really are under water, aren't we?"

"Sure are. They chained a few of us once and took us camping along the borderlands. I saw the dome for myself and the sea creatures." Lysander looked at her and motioned her over. "Come lay down by me and get some sleep. You look like you are about ready to collapse. They should not be back for a while. This is the time of day they like to pamper themselves, brushing each other's hair and singing compliments about each other's beauty."

Cassandra eyed him warily. He pulled back a blanket and patted the bed.

"Come on. I will not bite unless ordered to." There was sadness to his joke, but he managed a smile. "And only if they are looking."

There was really nowhere else in the cave room to go but the bed. Cassandra crossed over and sat on the end. Lysander turned his back on her. She looked over his loincloth covering his very nice ass. He was handsome, but her body longed for Iason.

"I am in love, too, you know," he said sadly.

"Surface world?"

"No, an Olympian. But what I feel is forbidden. Nothing will ever come of it."

"I'm in love with a Merr," Cassandra whispered, moving to lie down. She'd seen the look Neda had given them. Was that who he was talking about? Part of her waited for him to roll over and attack. He did not. Though, if he was going to force her, he wouldn't have had to lure her to lie next to him. He would have been able to force her wherever he wanted in the small room. She tried to relax, but it was difficult.

"The Merr?" Lysander sounded surprised. "But, we have been told they are worse than the Olympians."

"Not that I have seen," Cassandra said. "I have been with the Merr for a while now, well one of them at any rate, and if I had to choose, I would rather be there than here."

"Huh," Lysander whispered. Glancing over his shoulder, he said, "Get some sleep while you can. Trust me, you will be glad you did. As their newest addition, who knows what games they have in store for you?"

CHAPTER 21

CASSANDRA DIDN'T SLEEP as she listened to Lysander's soft, rhythmic snoring by her side. How could she rest when her mind raced with all that had happened to her? What if the underwater world was true? Lysander claimed to have seen it for himself— not that she trusted him. Though, he was human and it did give them a sort of companionship. If Iason hadn't been mistaken when he told her about Ataran being cast underneath the waves by an angry god, then maybe he wasn't mistaken about other things.

She thought over their time together and instantly blushed. Okay, so the sex part was wonderful and they'd done a lot of that, but he'd also shown himself to be a man of his word. He was respectful and kind. He never raised a hand to her or did anything she didn't ask of him—even if she only asked him with her body. True, she hadn't seen him away from his home and around others, but she felt as if she knew him. When he was around, she was happy. He was honorable and gentle and always treated her like a true princess.

Then, why on earth had she run away from him? Was she so scared of letting him love her? Was she scared of loving him back?

A sound outside the door startled her from her thoughts before she could draw any real conclusions. Lysander tensed, his snores stopping. He instantly turned, rolling over onto her body. His hand covered her mouth as she tried to scream in surprise at the sudden attack. She felt him pull the loincloth from his hips and toss it aside.

"You'd best pretend like I've just spent the last hour fucking you into submission," he hissed in her ear, "or they'll whip us both and give you to the other slaves. Trust me, the others will not have a choice but to subdue you because Maia will watch to make sure her orders are followed."

The door was pushed open before she could answer. Cassandra moaned weakly as he tore off his hand. Lysander snarled at her so the mermaid at the door could see before rolling off. It was one of the warrior Olympians in the loincloth and fur bra. Lysander looked at the door, affecting an expression of complete dispassion as he kneeled before the woman.

"My queen," Lysander said. "I have done what you asked of me. She is subdued and will obey you."

Cassandra rolled onto her side, pulling the messed up bedding around her as she lifted her knees into her stomach. Curling into a ball, she made a distressed, weak sound for effect.

"Ah, very good, slave," the mermaid answered, chuckling darkly. "You may rest now. We are very pleased with you."

"Thank you, my queen." Lysander bowed his head once more before walking back toward the bed. He glanced at Cassandra, his eyes pleading and sorrowful at the same time.

"Come, pet," the mermaid ordered. "Queen Maia would like to see you now."

Cassandra pretended to adjust her clothing beneath the bedding before standing. She walked slowly, making a stumbling arch around where Lysander was. The mermaid noticed this and nodded to herself in approval. Lysander managed a sad, quick lift of the corner of his mouth as she left him.

Cassandra followed the mermaid captor from the slave's room, waiting as the woman locked Lysander back inside. The mermaid motioned that she was to follow her back to the front part of the cave. She did so without speaking. Keeping her head bowed, she watched her feet.

Queen Maia sat on a throne, as if waiting for Cassandra. The mermaid who'd led her from the room pushed her down on her hands and knees before the queen. The hard stone scraped her skin, and she moaned lightly.

"It is done," the mermaid that fetched her from Lysander's room said. "He was still going at her when I arrived."

Several of the listening mermaids laughed.

"Lysander always did have stamina," Maia said.

Cassandra glanced up only to feel her head being pushed rudely down from behind.

"No, let her look at my beauty." Maia said. When Cassandra again lifted her eyes, the queen continued. "Do you still love the Merr?"

Cassandra glanced around the cave before again eyeing the queen. Did Maia think she'd answer that question honestly? Instinctively knowing what the woman wanted to hear, she lied. "No."

"Ah, good." Maia nodded in approval. There was

a strange tension in the room, an anger that lay underneath all the smug smiles and beautiful eyes. "I knew you would enjoy the rough force of our slave. Once you had a taste of something," she paused in thought, giggling to herself. "Shall we say, better than a Merr man? You soon learn that love is an illusion of sex, and one male's tools work as well as the next one's."

Cassandra didn't move, didn't speak. There was nothing she could say to the demented mermaid queen.

"You know, we had a human here not too long ago." Maia stood. "Do you know her? Bridget."

Cassandra tensed. Bridget had been here? How? Iason said the woman was at the Merr palace with another hunter, Caderyn.

"We should have forced her to stay with us, forced her into a slave's bed so that she felt the pleasures we have to offer. Instead, she escaped us, running back to her Merr lover." Maia frowned, and it spread like a wave over the others' faces. "I was not about to make the same mistake with you."

"What do you want with me?" Cassandra asked, looking up as Maia came to stand before her. Maia motioned and two mermaids hauled her to her feet.

"Lady Bridget's body had changed so now she is

one of us. We tried to drown her, but the gods chose to bless her. We wanted her to join us," Maia paused. She touched Cassandra's cheek lightly, caressing it. There was nothing sexual in the way the mermaids touched her. It was more like she was their new toy—an oddity they wanted to play with, a mere doll to fondle and dress up. An almost desperate boredom seeped from each and every one of them.

"You do not have to be a prisoner of Atlas," Lotis said, coming up behind Maia and resting a hand on her shoulder. The woman's red coloring was just spooky, like some Hollywood horror costume designed to frighten little children. "You do not have to be their slave. Here you can have many slaves. Here you can be a queen."

"If you are one of us, you will be free," a dark haired temptress said, coming up behind Cassandra. She stood close to her back.

"You will come and go as you please," Maia added. "You may take your pleasures from the slaves. They will obey you. You may take as many as you want to your bed, so long as you do not take them all at the same time."

Cassandra tried to politely edge away from the woman behind her, but it was clear they weren't into allowing for personal space.

"We will not let you be a prisoner of Atlas." Maia closed her eyes, smiling slightly. "They made you come here, didn't they? They forced you, and now they will tell you to choose a mate so that you may spend your days subservient to them."

Cassandra thought of the male slaves these women kept. Even if what they said was true, they were hypocrites.

"But, I'm human," Cassandra whispered. Her heart called out for Iason. She was terrified. There was no way around it. At least Bridget had escaped them. And, if Bridget escaped, then she would too.

"That will determine it, of course," Lotis said, nodding.

"Determine what?" Cassandra continued to edge away. For some reason, she wanted to keep Lotis at the farthest distance.

"Well," Maia laughed. "If the gods have blessed you as they have us, the water won't kill you and our offer will give you something to think about as you are reborn. But, if they have not blessed you, then what's the death of one mortal to us?"

Laughter sounded, echoing in the cave. Hands grabbed her, pulling her toward the cave pond. Cassandra screamed, kicking and pleading, but there were just too many of them.

"Join us," Maia said. "Or you will die. Unfortunately, the choice is not really yours."

Several of the women dove into the water. When they surfaced, they stretched out their arms in waiting. Cassandra gasped as she was dragged across the ground. The harder she struggled, the harder they laughed at her efforts. Lysander had been right. These women were incredibly strong.

"May the gods be with you!" Maia called on her way back to her throne. "Because no one else will."

The mermaids tossed her over the side of the pool. Her limbs flailed in the air. As she splashed beneath the icy surface, salt water gushed into her mouth. Instantly, the mermaids in the water grabbed hold of her, keeping her down. She fought them, scratching and biting anything she could reach. But, after a few hard, solid punches to her stomach, Cassandra was forced to gasp in sea water. It choked her lungs. She thought of Iason, wanting him, missing him, needing him.

Cassandra's lungs filled with the heavy liquid. Fingers gripped her tightly about the legs and arms, dragging her down. Her entire body burned for a second and then it was over. Blackness consumed her and all was dark.

IASON GRABBED HIS CHEST, feeling a wave of pain wash over him. Cassandra? He could almost hear her in his head, calling to him, needing him. He had discovered some tracks in the forest, but they were hard to follow. Running, he used his instincts instead, trying to sense where she was. He had to find her. He had to get to her. Gods only knew what the Olympians were doing to her.

"Poseidon, please, I beg you. Help me. Without her, I am nothing. Do not send her to me only to take her away."

CHAPTER 22

Iason! Iason, help me! Please, I need you.

Cassandra jerked, but her limbs were stuck. Pressure caved in her chest. She could barely move. Her eyelids were too heavy to open, and she felt cold—so very cold. There was something around her wrists, holding her down. She struggled against the ties. Her eyes popped open, and she automatically tried to breathe.

She was underwater, her wrists bound to keep her down beneath the surface. Cassandra opened her mouth wide, trying to take air into her lungs, fighting for breath. It was no use. Her lungs were full of unmoving salt water. She pulled at her wrists, rubbing them raw against the ties. The salt water stung the wounds, but she didn't care. She had to get to the surface. She needed air.

Her muscles were stiff and sore and she had to stop struggling. She closed her mouth, hoping to get the briny taste of the ocean off her tongue. As she floated, suspended in the water, she slowly calmed as she realized the sharp pain of drowning was gone. Something fluttered on her neck, seeming to pull in water. The burning in her chest lessened with each pull. Her eyes saw clearly in the dark depths of the pond. Looking around, she realized she was alone. Above her, she saw the waving pattern of the cave ceiling, but there was no one watching her. Below her, the pond went deep.

Her wrists were bound with what looked like seaweed, keeping her under the surface. Then, seeing her green tail, she stiffened. That is why she couldn't move her legs. They were gone. She was a mermaid.

For a long, stunned moment, Cassandra couldn't rationalize what was happening. Iason had been telling the truth. She was destined to become a mermaid.

She glanced at her forearms. Two small, green fins had formed there. They had small swirls in them like the surface of a sea shell, just like Iason's. She felt the water brushing up against them, just as she felt it almost vibrating along her new tail. They were part of her. Her tail was skinnier than Iason's, the split along the bottom longer as it parted into two fins. The ends fluttered in the water like wet silk.

Cassandra forced her panic aside. She was naked, her dress gone. Her red hair drifted around her in the water. She tried to move, but it was a little awkward when her tail swished back and forth. Concentrating, she did it again, trying to learn about her new body. The cool water against her scales felt odd, so sensitive to the most subtle shift of the currents and temperatures, but not uncomfortably so. It was as if her internal thermometer had reset itself.

Pulling her arms, she worked her way down so that the wrist straps were loose in the water. She glanced up, still no one. It took a while of pulling, but she managed to get free by cutting the seaweed with the hard fins on her forearms.

Cassandra bit her lip. Did she swim up, or did she look for another way out? She glanced around the pond, using her new eyesight to cut through the black water as she searched for a way to escape. Seeing a dark hole toward the bottom, she swam down. It was a little awkward, but she managed to get to it. Peeking through the hole, she saw a long underwater tunnel. It was slow going, but she refused to give up. Using her arms and new tail, she managed to work her way through the tight hole to an open seabed. She couldn't see any mermaids so she slowly pushed through the tunnel's opening. An underwater field spread out before her, covered with gently flowing sea grass.

The Abyss.

There was no question in her mind as she looked around the wide expanse of water. She blinked several times, struggling to control her fin as she floated in the water. It was dark, but she could see clearly in the icy depths. All around her was silence. She was in Deep Ocean—a place no mortal could go. Just like the seashore above, the sea stretched on into the distance. She shivered, feeling very small in comparison. Cassandra looked up, detecting a tiny, wormlike creature swimming several feet overhead. Though it was tiny around, it was incredibly long. She moved her hands, slowly pushing her body down, away from the creature. There were creatures down here no mortal person had ever seen, and the worm was probably the least of her concerns.

Cassandra turned around, gripping to the wall outside the Olympian's cave entrance. She hugged her body against it, finding some small comfort in a stationary hold. Did she risk getting lost in the ocean? Or did she go back inside and face the crazed women? Remembering Lysander's words, she knew that either fate could end horribly.

A dome.

Lysander said that the borderlands were a dome overlooking the ocean. So, if she were to find the dome, perhaps she could see in just as the Merr and Olympians could see out. It was worth a try.

Cassandra looked around. A small creature peeked its head up from the sandy ocean floor. The translucent body was eerie and it had long claws, like a giant lobster. She pulled herself up the rocky incline, away from the terrifying shellfish. Who knew what dangers lurked in these waters? One thing she did know was that dangers also awaited her in the Olympian's den. If she was going to escape capture, she'd need to hurry.

'Iason,' she thought, trying to call to him. Cassandra used her arms to pull her body up the side of the rock cliff, working away from the cave. Iason had mentioned telepathy when they swam in water and it couldn't hurt to try using it now. If anything, talking to him would make her feel like she wasn't so alone. *'Honey, if you hear me, please come and get me now. I don't like it out here.'*

Iason stopped, tilting his head to the side. He was so frustrated that his whole body shook. There was no doubt in his mind that he would find the Olympian's hideout, but it was slow going. Thoughts of what could be happening to Cassandra filled his head. Who knew what the crazy women were doing to her. It had been so long since any of them had seen Maia and her mermaid followers.

'Iason.'

He heard it again. Cassandra was calling out to him. Her voice was distant, faint.

'Iason...please...don't like it out here.'

He tensed. Where was she? He listened harder, but there was no more. What were those accursed sea witches doing to her? Why could she speak telepathically to him? Unless...

"She's changed," Iason whispered, wondering if the Olympians had tried to drown Cassandra only to watch her turn into Merr form. Was it possible they now kept her locked beneath the water in a cage? The rumors about what Queen Maia was capable of were horrible, nightmarish tales.

He growled in frustration, not knowing in which direction to run. Cassandra needed him and he was failing her. Closing his eyes, he tried to calm his beating heart, but it was impossible. He wanted her back in the safety of his arms. Why did she run from him? Why couldn't he have known she would? He shouldn't have told her they were married.

'*Cassandra,*' he said, using his mind to call out to her. '*Cassandra, answer me. Please, answer me. Tell me how I can find you. Show me the way.*'

CHAPTER 23

CASSANDRA WASN'T sure how much time had passed, but it felt like she'd spent an eternity down in the ocean's depths. Her stomach was sore from swishing her tail so she used her arms instead, pulling herself along the rocky protrusion.

'*I should have done more stomach crunches in my workouts,*' she thought, trying not to tighten the sore muscles. '*Okay, I should have actually worked out.*'

She was sure she could have made better time in the open ocean, if she would have been a better swimmer, but she was too scared to brave the waters in her new body. Besides, there was some comfort in the solid feel of rock beneath her hands. What if a current came along and swept her away from the dome. Alone, unable to find Iason or the Merr people, floating in an endless sea, did not sound like the way she wanted to spend the rest of her life.

So far, she'd been lucky and had only seen a few large creatures in the distance and a smattering of smaller ones crawling along the ocean floor. Unfortunately, the best of her eyesight was extremely tunneled and she had to constantly move her head around to see in all directions. No wonder Iason had such a strong neck. Her muscles ached and were beginning to stiffen. Every once in a while, she would get a sense that something was near her and knew which way to look.

Seeing a soft glow breaking through the eternal darkness of the Abyss, she hurried forward. Could that be the dome? In her excitement, she renewed her efforts, swimming hard toward it. She moved upward, desperate for the light.

Then, without warning, a sudden gush of water rushed past her back fin, sending her into a spiral. As she turned in the water, she saw a long, worm-like creature, only it wasn't like a tiny earthworm found in a garden, or even the thin, long worm she'd seen earlier. This one was as big as a subway and just as fast. Pumping her arms, she righted herself in the water. The creature's movement had thrown her away from the rock face and left her in open terrain.

'*Shit! Oh, no, no, no.*' Cassandra worked her arms, trying to swim in a straight line. Her movements were wobbly, but she managed to make some progress. A tingling erupted over her, and she turned in time to see the worm's giant head coming right for her. The creature didn't have a face, but instead a gelatinous-like mouth in the center of the rounded tip. She opened her mouth to scream, but no sound came out under the water. However, she did hear the sound reverberating in her head. '*Ahh!*'

Cassandra pumped her arms harder, trying to get away. Feeling a suctioning sensation by her tail, she turned and hit the creature with her arm, cutting it with her fin. The worm let go of her, falling slightly. She darted toward the light, twisting and turning in the water to get to safety.

As she approached it, glancing back to make sure she wasn't being followed, she realized that she had indeed found the dome. Darkness no longer pervaded as she swam into the softened glow. It looked like an enormous bubble, trapped at the bottom of the sea. Desperate, she hurried forward, as if she could swim right through the barrier. Reaching out, her hand struck the smooth surface and slid. She crashed into the hard side.

'No!' She hit the dome. 'No, *let me through. Damn it, I do not want to stay in the water!*'

Cassandra began to cry. She'd been brave up until that moment. But now, seeing the blurry shift of a forest, she couldn't hold back. All the desperation and fear she felt came to the surface. She pushed at the dome. Land was so close, just on the other side of the barrier, but she couldn't get to it. She was like a fish, pressed against the glass of the fishbowl, unable to swim into the distance.

She looked up. The dome only disappeared into darkness, leading into what was the Merr's sky. Even if she was to swim up, there wouldn't be a way in. So, what did she do? Go back to the outcropping of rock that held the world above the true ocean floor like a pedestal? Did she try to find an opening to let her in? Iason had mentioned the palace opening being the only way in or out. Obviously, she'd found another opening through the Olympian's cave, did that mean there were more the Merr didn't know about? What were the odds that she would make it to the opening at Atlas? As large as the dome was, it was like looking for an orange buried somewhere in Australia. The odds were definitely against her. If the worm didn't find her first, then any number of things could come for her—including the Olympians.

Why did she leave Mt. Olympus? Surely it was safer than dying alone in the dark ocean. Why did she leave Iason's home. She was happy there. She was happy with him. Why did she have to run?

'Iason, I'm sorry. Please find me. I need you. Please, I do not want to be out here anymore.'

CHAPTER 24

'*AHH!*'

Iason froze, his whole being tense as he waited for another sound. Cassandra's fear washed over him, and he felt her as surely as he felt himself. He waited, desperate for word, desperate to connect with her and be able to speak, desperate for a hint of where she was so he could rescue her.

'*Talk to me Cassandra,*' he thought. '*Hear me. Come on, hear me. Tell me where you are.*'

'*Let me through.*' He heard her voice clearer than before.

The fact that her telepathy was getting clearer told him she had definitely changed. He was thankful for that. In their vanity over being immortal, Queen Maia and her followers would be less likely to harm her now that she was like them. It would be a lot harder to kill her too.

'Damn it, I do not want to stay in the water!'

The water? The Olympians had her under water? The closest salt water pond that he knew of, other than the one on his land, was on Caderyn's land. That had to be where they had taken her. Of course! What other place to make her shift than in a salt pond? His friend lived closer to the borderlands, not far from where he was. It was the best clue he had so far.

Iason started to run. He'd been up for hours, running about the countryside, but he wasn't tired. Cassandra needed him and he needed her. He would run until the end of time to get her back.

'Please, I do not want to be out here anymore. Stupid dome, let me in.'

Dome? Iason stopped. Cassandra was by the dome? But... how?

He looked up at the sky, to the barrier that protected them from the ocean's cold water. She was his wife. They should be connected. If she accepted him, if she called back to him, they should be able to communicate. Concentrating on the outside wall, he re-directed his thoughts in its direction, sending them toward the outer ocean beyond the barrier, *'Hear me, Cassandra, hear me.'*

'Iason?' The sound was faint, but the voice belonged to a woman. It had to be his Cassandra.

'Aye, it's me. Where are you? What happened?' Iason's whole body tensed. He wanted to hold her, to feel her, but rejoiced in the knowledge that she was alive. There was still time to save her. He stopped running, breathing hard as he turned in circles, as if by doing so he would suddenly find her before him.

'Iason! Argh, I hate this mind-telepathic thing. I will never get it. Iason, are you out here? Caderyn is looking for you!'

'Who are you?' Iason demanded, frowning.

'Bridget, Caderyn's wife.'

Bridget? The human woman Caderyn had saved? What was she doing out here? And did she say she was Caderyn's wife?

'Caderyn,' he heard Bridget say, *'I have him in my head, now what?'*

'Where in all the ocean is he?' Caderyn asked.

'Caderyn?' Iason glanced around but didn't see anyone. *'Where are you?'*

'Iason? By all the ocean creatures, man! Where have you been? We've been running around the forest all night trying to find you. Olympians have been

detected out in the ocean. King Lucius has ordered us to bring the human in your care back to Atlas where it is safe for her. We feared that they might try to harm...'

'It's too late,' Iason said. *'Cassandra is gone.'*

"Gone?" Bridget demanded, no longer using the telepathic link. "What do you mean she's gone?"

Iason spun on his heels. The woman looked much healthier than when he last saw her, even out of breath as she was from running.

Caderyn appeared behind her. Instantly, he saw a different light in his friend's eyes. They were content, happy, renewed. "Olympians tried to kidnap Bridget. We sent word from Atlas, but your caretakers said the messenger never arrived. Then, when a Merr woman was reported in the water, we knew we had to come and tell you ourselves as we never received word from you. We believe the Olympians have found a way to breathe surface air, and they also have a way out into the water."

"I know." Iason was glad to see his friend there and was even relieved somewhat by Bridget's presence. She was from Cassandra's time and would know how Cassandra would think and act. "They took Cassandra. I was looking for their lair, but..." He looked back at the dome. "I think she has escaped them."

"Escaped?" Bridget asked.

Iason shared a look with his fellow hunter. He wasn't sure how much Bridget knew, but since she was using telepathy, he could only assume she knew about her fate as a mermaid, and had in fact gone through the change herself. "Into the water. I think the Olympians drowned her and she somehow got out into the abyss."

"Her, too?" Bridget asked. She shook her head, frowning in displeasure. "Those stupid bitches pulled me under as well. What is their problem anyway? You don't see me trying to jerk them into the surface air to see if they'll live, do you?"

Iason started to answer, but Caderyn held up his hand. "She knows the story. She's just venting about them. Give her a moment and she'll stop."

"What if Cassandra was the Merr woman the guard worm detected in the water? You know, when he was mind jabbering on about it?" Bridget asked. "What if she was trying to escape the creature? If I saw a giant worm in the water, I'd try to stab it, too."

Iason's whole body was stiff. Unless a Merr knew how to communicate to the worm, it wouldn't take kindly to an intruder's presence. The creature was thousands of years old and had taken up residence under the platform beneath Ataran. But the worm was hardly the most dangerous thing in the Abyss. As he was a hunter, he knew how to navigate the waters and did so naturally. He knew which beasts to stay away from, how to act before others. Swimming in the ocean was second nature to him, but for Cassandra? She wouldn't know what to do.

As if voicing his fears, Bridget said, "The poor woman. She's out of her element in the abyss."

"I need to find her," Iason said.

"She didn't even make that great of a scientist," Bridget continued in deep thought. "The more I think about it, the more I'm becoming to believe that she didn't have a reason to be on the ship—not a scientific one anyway. Our expedition leader defended her, but I doubt she was a scientist at all, let alone someone with a working knowledge of the deep ocean."

"I do not think that's helping," Caderyn told his wife softly.

"What?" Bridget's eyes met Iason's and instantly she looked sorry. "You and Cassandra?"

"She is my wife," Iason said, unashamed. She might have run from him, might not fully accept their fate together, but that didn't stop the truth of what they were to each other.

"Oh," Bridget gasped, only to repeat, "oh."

"You stay here and try to call to her," Caderyn said. "We'll go back to Atlas and get in the water."

"I should come with you," Iason said, desperate to be in the water, but still not completely sure that was where his wife was.

"The king won't let you go," Caderyn said. "You have been with a sick human. They'll want to make sure nothing is wrong with you. Besides, she's new to the ocean, and she knows you. Try to find her along the borders, and direct her toward Ataran, to where we can find her. Tell her to stay in the dome's light."

Iason weakly nodded. It would take them about a day to get back from where they were if they ran full tilt. However, if they got close enough to the palace, they could send a telepathic call over the remaining distance and get the other hunters into the water searching.

"And, Iason," Caderyn said, putting his hand on his friend's arm. "Trust us, your friends, to bring your wife back safely."

CHAPTER 25

'Cass-an-dra,' the sing-song voice of the Olympians followed her. They were in her head, blocking out every other thought with the sound of their voices. Hours were filled with their taunts, their pleas, their offers to join their band of psychotic warrior queens, until finally a day had passed. She did her best not to answer the call, not to have a coherent, conscious thought, not to slip and let them track her through the dark abyss, but it became increasingly harder. 'Cass-an-dra, where are you?'

'Leave me alone,' she thought. Every muscle in her ached as she clung to the rocky protrusion molded to the dome of Ataran.

'Oooh, we hear you again, Cassandra, sweet Cassandra,' Queen Maia's voice rose above the others, growing stronger. 'You cannot escape us, Cassandra. We are in your head now. You are one of us. Come back, the ocean is no place for a new little mermaid like you, but we can teach you. We can show you, Cassandra. Come back to us, and we promise not to punish you for running away. We know you were just scared. But there is nothing to be afraid of. We can help you. Come back to us. Come back to us.'

The words drifted like the currents all around her. Cassandra was so tired of running from them and Iason did not come for her, though she'd been too scared to call out to him for fear that the Olympians would hear her. She wasn't exactly sure how the telepathy thing worked. Could everyone hear her thoughts? How did she block out those she didn't want to hear? Everything she did, trying to avoid talking to the Olympians, seemed to fail. And exactly how well could they track her with just her thoughts?

'Come back to us, Cassandra, come back...'

Her heart raced as she tried to force her body on, but the flips of her tail had grown weak. It was possible she'd missed the entrance to Atlas or wasn't even close. It wasn't as if there were big road signs showing how many more miles she had to swim before she reached her destination. Cassandra missed signs. She missed civilization and land. She missed her grandmother, fast food, dry clothes and sunlight. Those were the things she thought about in her ordeal as she tried to keep herself sane. And the one thing she tried hardest not to think about was Iason the Hunter.

CHAPTER 26

SHE COULDN'T GO ON. If her face wasn't already wet, tears would have streamed down her cheeks. With her cancer, Cassandra was used to pain, but this was different. This was emotional agony, helplessness and fear like she'd never felt before. If someone would have asked her right after her diagnosis if she could ever feel anything more frightening, she would have said no.

And she would have been wrong.

More and more, a gentle stirring seemed to try and pull her away from the dome. She closed her eyes, allowing her body to float, so tired she wanted to sleep forever. Only this time if she woke up to find Iason standing over her, offering every fantasy a woman could want, she wouldn't throw the chance away. Fear would not stop her from being with him.

'Iason,' she whispered, even her thoughts tired. *'I'm sorry I ran from you. Thank you for everything you did for me.'*

Silence filled her mind, answering her words. She wished he could hear them, could know that he made her last days so beautiful.

'It's funny. I don't feel sick anymore, but I'm dying anyway from exhaustion. Perhaps it was just fate that this is my time.' The smooth dome bumped her arm and a jagged rock touched her back. She was beginning to drift down toward the ocean floor. Even the thoughts of the translucent lobsters couldn't give her the willpower to move. Her body turned, and she felt the water passing over her arms faster than before. She felt like a feather. She was falling.

'Goodbye, Iason.'

Her body hit the ground, bouncing on the stiff sand before coming to rest. She turned her face to the side, her cheek pressed to the ground as she lay on her stomach. A soft smile curled her lips. No matter what happened now, she'd already seen more in her short life than many others before her had. She had seen solid proof that the supernatural existed. And, she had felt love. What more could a person ask for?

'*Goodbye, Iason, goodbye,*' she thought.

"GOODBYE?" Iason panicked, running his hands along the dome's border as he searched for his wife. The borderlands went on for miles, but she had to be near. He had to find her. '*Cassandra? What do you mean goodbye?*'

The mind link had been quiet as he walked along the border, trying to sense the water. He could detect plenty of sea creatures in the abyss, but no Cassandra. Or, if she was there, she wasn't moving. Iason stepped around a tree that pressed along the dome.

'*Cassandra, my sweet little sea flower, please, answer me.*'

Afternoon faded to evening and evening to night. There was a subtle shifting of colors across the sky. The sea stars came toward the dome, drawn to the heat as they danced around the dark blue-black. The seas stars were actually little glowing fish a little smaller than his hand. Their black eyes followed him, watching him hurry past. Occasionally, the lights would part, showing a black streak going across as creatures swam past, but the streaks were never his wife.

'*Cassandra,*' Iason called, over and over, '*Cassandra!*'

He ran his hand over the moist dome, swiping against it. The little creatures jolted, parting to show him the darkness beyond, but soon settled as they got used to his nearness. Iason continued on, repeating the motion with a new set of stars, again watching them scatter so he could peek out into the dark ocean beyond.

'*Cassandra!*'

Iason closed his eyes, concentrating, hoping against hope that he could sense the guard worm and communicate with it. The creature didn't answer, not that he expected it to. A large squid zoomed overhead, and his stomach tensed to see it. Normally, they were just big pests, but to Cassandra they'd be dangerous. The creature's body drifted by slowly— first its large eyes, then its gelatinous body, its arms, and finally its two large tentacles.

'*Away,*' Iason yelled at it, jumping to jolt it away. '*Away!*'

The trees cleared, giving him more room. He hurried along, reaching out toward her. Desperation and fear overwhelmed him. She'd said goodbye. He heard it in his head.

'*Not goodbye,*' he told her, begging her to hear. He pounded the dome. "Not goodbye!"

CHAPTER 27

CASSANDRA JOLTED, blinking rapidly. When she fell, she hadn't bothered to look where she landed, not wishing to know. Now, she opened her eyes to see one of the translucent lobsters sitting right in front of her face, staring at her. Its pinchers opened and shut lightly and its feelers drifted.

'*Ugh.*' She pushed up, sitting on the bottom of the ocean floor. How long had she slept?

By the feel of her limbs, it hadn't been long enough. The end of her tail fluttered in the water when she moved. Looking up, she detected large jellyfish overhead, spinning gracefully in a swarm as they pumped rhythmically through the water. Their bodies held an inner light that illuminated down their streamer-like tentacles. The giant lobster just sat, not bothering her. It really was beautifully serene, once she paid attention.

'*Cassandra!*'

Cassandra blinked. '*Great, now I'm hallucinating. At least it's Iason's voice and not the Olympians.*'

'*Cassandra?*'

'*Iason?*' She pushed up, swimming without thought of her exhaustion. '*Iason, where are you? I hear you.*'

As she passed the rocky ledges, she saw the dome swarming with glowing star-shaped fish. She hesitated, not sure if it was safe to get too close. Dots of light reflected off her body and spotted the ocean behind her.

'*Cassandra, I'm here. I can't see you.*' He sounded panicked but close.

'*Where?*' She worked her arms in a circle, checking her surroundings. '*Are you in the ocean? Did you find your way through the Olympians' cave? I'm so happy to hear your voice. I hate being alone out here. Where are you?*'

'*The dome.*' His voice was saddened.

Cassandra turned, her hair floating in a red cloud around her as she looked toward the dome. The glowing star fish scattered briefly and settled.

'*Come to the dome,*' Iason said. '*They won't hurt you.*'

Cassandra obeyed, eyeing the fish cautiously as she swam forward. A hand swiped by on the other side, and she caught a glimpse of emerald eyes. Reaching out, she pressed her hand to the glass. Iason found her, pressing his hand to hers on the other side. Though they couldn't touch, she felt his heat, felt him there.

Her eyes wide, she flicked her tail, pushing forward. The star fish scattered, unveiling his handsome face. Her heart skipped in her chest, like the first time she saw him, standing by the pond, about ready to dive beneath the waves. The brilliant green of his eyes shone as he searched her face. She pushed closer to the dome, her tail drifting down so her body was parallel to his.

The light from the sea stars danced over him, almost like soft disco lights over the muscular folds of his tight body. His chest was bare, his blond locks tangled and wild. He was perfection. A single strip of material covered his waist, tied haphazardly as if he'd dressed in a hurry. Remembering how she ran out on him, she glanced away.

'*Cassandra?*' The sound was hesitant.

She turned to him once more, trying to think of

what to say. So much had happened in such a short time. Her heart fluttered nervously as his eyes roamed over her.

'*You are beautiful,*' he said, his hand still pressed to hers.

IASON STARED AT HIS WIFE, her red hair floating around her like fine sea grass. Relief washed over him, making it hard to think beyond her beauty. She didn't move, didn't speak as she stared at him. Her eyes glowed more than before, the green brilliant as it reflected the sea stars' light. He had seen many mermaids and none had ever looked as lovely as she did right now. Her hand stayed on his, and he saw her green fin along her forearm, small and delicate. There were more white than green threads present within the shell pattern. Her bowed lips didn't part, but the small gills on her neck fluttered rapidly. She was nervous and had yet to control her breathing in the water.

Lowering her chin, she drifted closer, her face nearly pressing to the dome as she lifted her other hand to rest against it. Her hair floated around her shoulders, revealing her naked breasts. His eyes drifted to them and he swallowed over the liquid desire he felt surging through his veins. She was so close, he wanted to touch her, but there was no breaking through the barrier—not that he'd want to break through and flood his world.

Her narrow waist tapered down into a long, green and white tail. The caudal fin along the bottom was longer than his, the wet silk of it drifting far to the sides. He pressed his free hand to the glass, touching both of hers. Silvery green scales accented her eyes as she again looked away. She seemed so sad.

'*Cassandra? Are you hurt?*' he asked at length when she didn't speak.

She shook her head no.

'*Are you...?*' He closed his eyes, pressing his forehead to the dome near hers. She drifted down lower to be more at his eye level. '*Are you angry with me still?*'

Again, she shook her head in denial.

'*Will you speak to me?*' His nose brushed along hers, not able to feel more than her heat.

'*I was frightened,*' she said, her eyes wide.

'*I know. I'm sorry. I didn't know the Olympians had ventured into the forest. They hadn't been out for so long. And we didn't know they had a way into the water, or else we would have blocked it. I know you* were scared. I should have been there for you. I should have protected you. It is my duty to keep you safe, and I failed you.'

'No, no.' She shook her head in denial. 'I should never have run away. I was frightened when you said I was your wife. I saw that you cared for me, because a man like you would never take a wife he did not care for.'

'And you did not care for me?' Pain rippled over him and his hands dropped some.

'I care too much.'

He swore he heard tears in her voice. 'I do not understand. Then, why run?'

'The last thing I wanted was to hurt you, Iason. You have given me so much, more than anyone else in my life has ever done.'

'So you ran? That is how you don't hurt me? By running away?'

'I'm dying, Iason. I ran away because I'm dying, and there is no cure for what I have.' Her head moved back and forth, as if grinding her forehead into the dome. He saw the white spot where her flesh pressed hard. 'I might be dying still. I honestly don't know. The doctors on the surface call it cancer. I have already outlived all of their expectations, but it is taking me. The night you saved me from the shipwreck, I had prepared myself to die. I could barely move. The pain was too much and I was ready to let go. But then I awoke and I wasn't dead and though I still felt pain, I felt something else—a desire to live no matter the suffering. I felt you, Iason. I felt your love for me. That is why I never let you say it. I did not want to make you love me only to lose me. I care for you too much. I love you too much.'

'You did not make me love you, Cassandra. I love you freely. Nothing can change that. The gods have given you to me.'

'Only to take me away?' Again she looked away, and he felt her anguish. 'I cannot do that to you. I do not want to hurt you. I'm scared, Iason. I've never wanted to live so badly. I've never had so many reasons to fight for. If I can't... If I don't...'

'The Merr do not suffer from human illnesses. You are not going to die. Not that way.' Iason smiled. She loved him. 'That is why Althea the Healer asked me to take you to the country so that I may heal you without anyone knowing. She felt the human medicine in you, felt your pain. I risked everything—my life, my reputation, my status as a Hunter—all for you. I even gambled my future by giving you so much of me. When I made you my wife without asking express permission, I broke our laws. I did it to save you, for *without you I am lost, I am nothing. I loved you the second you kissed me as I saved you. I had to save you. Why do you think you lived longer than they said you would? The gods were bringing you to me. Would you have gone to the ocean otherwise? Would you have accepted me? This is ordained, Cassandra.'*

'*You saved a stranger.'*

'*No, I saved the mate to my heart.'*

'*You broke no laws, then, my love,'* she whispered. '*For your heart asked mine and it said yes. A thousand, million times yes!'*

'*I want to hold you.'* He sighed, running his hands over her image. '*It's not safe in the ocean. You need to swim toward the palace.'*

'*I have been trying.'* Cassandra pressed her lips to the dome, her lids falling lazily over her eyes. '*I want to be with you.'*

'*I want you here.'* Iason leaned forward to kiss her through the barrier.

'*And I want a handkerchief,'* a voice sneered, '*to wipe away my happy tears.'*

Cassandra stiffened, turning.

'*What?'* Iason demanded. '*Who is it?'*

'*Maia,'* Cassandra whispered.

'*Maia'* Iason growled. '*Cassandra, swim! Do not let her catch you.'*

'*Too late, lover, I already see her,*' Maia laughed. '*Your pretty little wife is mine. By the time I let her go she won't even remember your name.*'

'*Cassandra,*' Iason yelled. '*Swim!*'

'*Cassandra,*' a voice taunted, different than Maia's.

'*Oh, Cassandra, run away from the naughty mermaids,*' another screamed in mock horror. Cackling laughter followed.

'*Swim, Cassandra.*'

'*Hurry.*'

'*Oh, poor Hunter, going to lose his wife to a bunch of wicked, naughty mermaids.*'

The taunts continued. Cassandra drifted back, as if inching away from the sound. Her fingers skimmed the glass, and she reached desperately for him, begging Poseidon to let the barrier open long enough to let her through unharmed.

'*Junia, Lotis, grab her,*' Maia ordered.

'*Iason?*' Cassandra said weakly. Her big green eyes met his for the briefest of moments.

A blur of movement scattered the sea stars. He yelled, pounding the dome as red fins dashed by like a striking shark. The mermaid knocked Cassandra in the waist, sending her tumbling away from his sight.

'*No!*' Iason ran along the dome, trying to scatter

the sea stars so he could see. They dissipated somewhat with the commotion on the other side and he focused, looking into the water. Without being in it, it was very hard to see into the depths. *'Cassandra? Speak to me. Cassandra!'*

Desperate to help her when she didn't answer, he tried to summon back the giant squid, hoping it was still in the water. If anything, maybe it would keep the Olympians occupied so Cassandra could escape. Maia would defend the prisoner only because it would please her vanity to own Cassandra when a Merr hunter wanted her. Closing his eyes, he concentrated on the sea. *'Come on, where are you? Come on...'*

CHAPTER 28

CASSANDRA FOUGHT LOTIS' hold on her, but it did little good. The mermaid was strong and had more control over the movements of her body. She heard Iason yelling for her, but she couldn't concentrate long enough to answer him. Whenever she tried, Junia would slap her with her tail. Flashes of red appeared in the spotted sea stars' light as she nearly freed herself from Lotis' tightening grip. The mermaids' cruel giggles clouded her head and Iason's screams stopped.

'Let me go!' Cassandra commanded, only to receive cackling laughter in response. A naked breast came close to her face and she grimaced, struggling to be free. A tail whacked her hard on her side.

'Electra, help them! Keep her still. Tie her arms so

we can drag her back to Olympia.' Maia demanded. Brown hair swarmed around Cassandra's face as Electra darted past them with rope. Someone grabbed her hands and the sea became a flurry of movement. 'Hurry it up. I feel a squid coming for us fast.'

'Cassandra?' Iason screamed. 'Try to hide. Something big is coming!'

Suddenly, a dark, black streak darted past. Cassandra blinked, thinking it either her imagination or another mermaid coming to help tie her.

'What was...?' Lotis began to screech.

'Who...?' Electra's cry joined her friend's. The black fin darted by again, and a red wound suddenly appeared on the mermaid's arm. 'Ah, it cut me!'

'Hunters,' someone shouted. It sounded like the Olympian Queen, but Cassandra couldn't be sure with the fear tainting the woman's words.

'Cassandra?' Iason called.

'We have her,' a man answered. 'Go to the palace, Iason. We will meet you there.'

'Maia,' a male voice growled so loud Cassandra's brain vibrated with the angry sound. 'How did you get out, you treacherous sea witch?'

'Solon?' Maia squeaked, only to order, 'Lotis grab her. Come on. We can outswim them.'

A flurry of fighting movement surrounded her as mermen darted in from the darkness, fins angled to fight as they took on the mermaids. They struck without mercy, and it was clear there were no tender sentiments about the females being the weaker sex. Though in truth, they didn't stand much of a chance against the bigger, stronger male hunters. The black tail swung out, striking Electra and sending her twirling back, head over tail, through the water. Lotis pulled on Cassandra's arm, her nails digging in hard as if to anchor her hold.

'*You bitch!*' Cassandra wrenched around in the water and punched Lotis in the nose as hard as she could. Her flesh made hard contact, and blood clouded the water. Lotis whimpered, and Cassandra drew back her hand to do it again. This time her fist glanced off the woman's cheek.

'*We have a fighter,*' a male voice yelled.

'*Iason has chosen well,*' another answered.

Lotis darted away.

'*Coward,*' Cassandra screamed after her.

'*Ow,*' one of the guys swore at her yell.

'*Easy with the mind link,*' another added.

'*This isn't over,*' Lotis hollered back, though she had disappeared into the dark distance.

'*I see we rescued you just in time,*' said a third male. '

Cassandra turned in the water at the comment, stopping as her vision focused on the black finned merman. Now that he hovered gently before her, she saw him clearly. She automatically pushed back. She thought Iason was big, but this man was huge. Her mouth worked before she shut it realizing she wasn't going to be able to speak that way.

'*Cassandra? Solon, is she hurt? I can't hear her.*' Concern rang in Iason's voice.

'*She is fine, my friend. Now run to the palace, we will meet you there.*'

'*A squid comes, you'd best hurry,*' Iason answered.

'*Brutus will see to it,*' Solon said. '*The sport will suit him.*'

'*Cassandra, I will see you at the palace. Go with them. They will protect you with their lives,*' Iason added, sounding a little further away. '*I love you.*'

She wanted to answer, but the big merman made her nervous and she felt too weak. Exhaustion seeped into every fin.

'*Demon, easy, you are scaring her.*' Another black finned merman appeared by Demon. They were identical in every aspect, from their long black hair to their matching dark eyes. Even their fins were the same silvery black color. Every subtle shift made them nearly invisible in the water. *'I managed to distract the squid by calling to some jellyfish. Though, we should go in case they try to migrate this way.'*

'I *think you are both scaring her,'* another said. His fins were green-gold and he was more Iason's size. She unconsciously inched more toward him but still didn't get too close. *'I am Solon of the Hunters. This is Demon and his brother, Brutus of the Warriors. They are hunters as well.'*

'Ca-Cass,' Cassandra managed, feeling light-headed. Her arms stung, and she looked down, surprised to find she'd been cut on the inside of her forearm.

'*She's hurt,'* Demon darted forward, capturing her up. His hand wrapped around her wounded limb, like a living bandage. *'Badly.'*

Cassandra felt her body being pulled with great speed through the water, as the merman held her arm tightly to keep it from bleeding. Her hair whipped against Demon's thick shoulder. Weakly, she said, *'You are a really big merman.'*

Brutus's chuckle sounded as her eyesight dimmed. Her wounded arm throbbed, and she let the darkness take her, too tired to do anything else.

CHAPTER 29

"BUTTERSCOTCH PUDDING!" Cassandra sat up, smacking her lips as she tried to scream her order out in the loud roaring of the diner. Taking a deep breath, she looked around. She wasn't in a diner filled with a crowd of people.

She was in a room on a low bed, next to another such bed. Light came from above, shining through decorative holes carved into the ceiling. The walls were smooth, almost adobe like in texture. Beautiful designs were painted directly on them. There was a small circular table in the corner with a pottery vase. It too was painted. A small stone desk stood in the corner. Rolled scrolls were places along the wall in diamond-shaped cubbies.

"This is the second time you have been in my care, my lady."

Cassandra blinked. A pretty woman walked in. She had kind eyes, the sort of eyes that reminded her of her grandmother. They had the same age to them, the gentle quietness. Though, this woman appeared younger and was thinner than her grandmother had been. Fine, draping material hung around her body, colored with the green-teal of the ocean. Two pins held the garment at the shoulders, leaving her arms bare. Her brown hair was pulled back from her face, fastened in an intricate coil around the crown.

"Second?" Cassandra asked.

"When you first came, the hunters brought you to my care."

"You are the healer. Althea." Cassandra remembered every word of her conversation with Iason. She glanced behind the woman, knowing before she looked that Iason was not behind her.

"I am, and you are in my home." The woman looked surprised. "You remember me? You were very sick the first time you came here and badly injured this second time.'

"I remember a feeling mostly. It reminded me of my grandmother taking care of me when I was sick, or when she came to me after her death in my dreams." Cassandra swung her feet over the side of the bed. She'd been dressed in a long white, wool tunica. The shapeless dress covered her arms, the loose material reaching from shoulder to feet. "It was warm and safe."

"I am honored to be in such a memory, my lady," Althea smiled kindly. "If you are up to visitors—?"

"Yes," Cassandra rushed. "Please send him in."

"Him?" Althea laughed. "No, I'm sorry. Iason has not arrived yet. I speak of Lady Bridget."

"Bridget?" Cassandra blinked in surprise. "Yes, of course. It'll be nice to see a familiar face."

Though, to be truthful, Bridget wasn't really an old friend. In fact, she always got the impression the woman didn't like her when they were on the ESC boat. The few times they had spoken to each other it had been tense. Of course, since she didn't know what she was doing as far as the scientific work went, it was no surprise Cassandra hadn't made that many friends. She became sad as she thought of Ned Devenpeck and the others drowning at sea.

"Althea said it was all right that I..." Bridget paused. "Are you well? Do you need me to get the healer?"

Bridget made a move to go. Cassandra quickly shook her head. "No, thank you, I'm fine. When the healer mentioned your name I couldn't help but think of," she shrugged her shoulder, unable to say their names, "the others."

Bridget nodded. "I understand. I like to think of them as safe, having been rescued by a passing ship. It's not very logical, but it makes me feel better."

"Bridget?" someone whispered. "Is it all right?"

Bridget glanced toward the door and laughed softly. "Cassie, this is Aidan Douglass."

A man leaned into the doorway, smiling. Short brown hair was slicked back on his head. He had kind brown eyes and an eager expression. "I have been waiting to meet you, Lady Cassie."

Cassandra smiled. "Me?"

"Aidan is a shipwreck survivor, like us," Bridget said.

"Well, not exactly like you. I've been here a little longer. I was born in eighteen-ninety-three in a southern county of Scotland." The man had a faint trace of a Scottish accent. "I was a historical scholar on my way to Africa to explore the great pyramids. I hoped to discover buried treasure. The boat I was on, the *Bella Donna*, was attacked and sank. Since there were no women onboard, I was saved and brought down."

"Aidan's a little touchy about the whole 'rescue the dames first' policy," Bridget said.

"And Bridget gets her back up when I mention how much more delicate females were in my time," Aidan said.

"You're a sloppy dresser," Bridget said, causing the man to look down over his loose wool pants and shorter wool shirt.

"And you're cursed with an overactive deductive reasoning," Aidan answered.

"I'm not a scientist," Cassandra offered, interrupting their banter.

Bridget's mouth opened as she turned to stare at Cassandra. Pointing, she gave a little jump. "I knew it!"

"I am so glad to hear it. Bridget has been useless when it comes to social information." Aidan's face became animated with excitement. "She's wonderful for scientific approaches and technological advances, but, well..."

"Just ask already," Bridget rolled her eyes.

"I can't wait to hear how the world has changed in the last hundred years," Aidan said. "I was wondering if you would mind coming to the artifacts room to discuss what you know about," he pointed toward the ceiling, "up there."

MICHELLE M. PILLOW

"Certainly," Cassandra said. "Though, I'm not sure how helpful I'll be. I left college early."

"I knew it," Bridget said again. Then, as if catching how rude she sounded, she added, "I didn't mean to imply that you were... I mean, I...I really want us to be friends. Can you just forget anything that comes out of my mouth that sounds rude or arrogant?"

"Sure," Cassandra laughed. "It feels good to be honest about not being a scientist. I hate science. I was more interested in the arts."

Aidan laughed. "That's exactly why I'd like your views on the surface world."

"He would like you to help out with cataloging knowledge, history, recovered artifacts, modern movies, stories, whatever you can remember. Basically, you dictate, he writes, and they send out a surface newsletter to everyone." Bridget grinned. "We get to live in the palace and be treated like princesses in exchange for remembering stuff."

"Yes, please," Aidan said.

Bridget giggled. "When I first arrived, I had to explain talking pictures to him."

"Talking pictures?" Cassandra shook her head, not understanding.

"Movies," Bridget said. "And he was most

concerned to know if we Americans had gotten our liquor back after the Prohibition."

"You must have a lot of questions," Aidan said, his tone hurried as he changed the subject. "I will be happy to answer them for you."

"We should..." Bridget motioned toward the door. "It would be more comfortable."

Cassandra followed the two of them to the other room. The healer was gone. Her home was a large square living area with low couches. Doors dominated most of the walls. There were a few closed doors, and an open, beaded door that led out to a hallway.

Althea didn't appear to be much for decoration. There were some paintings on the walls and minimal furniture. The low bench-like couches had no backs. Their wool seats were intricately woven and quite beautiful. The floors were bare, swept clean.

"I'm not sure what you've been told," Aidan began, not sitting. "But this world is, was, the ancient civilization of Atlantes. They call it Atlantes, not Atlantis like we do in the surface world."

"I know," Cassandra said.

"Oh." Aidan nodded. "Like all great civilizations, they became arrogant with power. Their vast empire ruled over much of the known world, such as Greece, Italy, Egypt—"

"I know," Cassandra said again. "Iason told me."

"He did?" Aidan almost looked disappointed.

"I believe he practices his speeches," Bridget explained.

"Then I suppose he told you about the curse and how none of us can ever set foot on mortal soil again?" Aidan sighed, as if disappointed.

Cassandra shook her head in denial. "Never?"

Aidan instantly perked up. "Poseidon cursed the people of Atlantes for their vanity and self-love. He granted them immortality, forever condemning them to walk on their earthly paradise and nowhere else. This land," as he spoke Bridget stood slightly behind him, her mouth moving to mimic his words, "he plunged into the water, trapping them so they could never set foot on mortal soil again. Here they have remained on the bottom of the ocean, their land drifting aimlessly with the currents. And now—"

"We are a part of it, never able to leave," Bridget finished for him.

He grinned, obviously enjoying the scholarly sparring. "Or, incidentally, breathe mortal air. It's one of the few things that will kill us."

Cassandra sat on the low couch. She looked at her hands, still feeling weak.

"We understand how overwhelming this can be," Aidan said. "I'm sure you have many more questions, and I will be happy to answer any of them."

"I do have one," Cassandra said, looking up at the two expectant faces.

"Yes?" they said in unison.

"Where is my husband?" Cassandra asked. "I really want to see him."

CHAPTER 30

IASON WAS BREATHLESS, but he didn't stop running as he entered the city of Atlas. His body was exhausted, and though he drew comfort from knowing his friends had found Cassandra, he would not feel better until he held her in his arms once more. Emotions crashed in on him like a tidal wave, making him feel more than he had in many years. He was exalted to be married to her, terrified at the thought of losing her, mystified by the idea that she could care for him, that she could love him.

The idea of her love made him run faster, up the slight hill to the palace, even as sweat seemed to pour off his body. Being a hunter, he had stamina and now that stamina was pushed to the limit. His heart beat hard and heavy in his chest, thundering violently in his ears, drowning out the greetings of those he passed. Iason was sure they would think him rude, but he could not be concerned with the thoughts of his fellow Merr. Not now. Not until he had Cassandra safe in his arms once more.

It was not lost on him how much his life had changed since that hunt when he'd saved her. Before, he'd been drifting along for centuries, his life an endless ocean. Aye, that ocean changed, different creatures, different currents, and yet it was always the same. And then Cassandra fell into the water, sending a ripple over him, vibrating him to his very being until he was ready to risk everything for her— the life he'd built as a hunter.

But what was that life without Cassandra? His Cassandra. His wife.

"Lord Iason!"

This was one voice he couldn't ignore, and he cursed inwardly at the palace gate. Bowing his head, he said a little too breathlessly, "King Lucius."

The king smiled, looking the hunter over with a small grin on his face. He had bright blue eyes and light brown hair that was longer than most, as it fell to his mid-back. "I see the rumors are true. The second of the three has been chosen."

Iason couldn't help the way the corner of his

mouth lifted. "Aye, my king, she has. Now, if you will excuse me, I'd like to—"

"I don't suppose this run of hunting luck will last and I can expect you to bring down more women, women who are free to choose beyond the hunters who saved them?" The king's eyes were sad, and Iason realized that the man had hoped, as they all secretly hoped, that one day the gods would choose them, would bless them with love, with a wife, with a family.

"Does this mean I have your blessing?"

"Does she agree?" the king asked.

Iason nodded.

"So be it." The king nodded. "You are married. I will announce it tonight as the hall dines. Please, come, if your bride is up to it. But, don't be surprised if there are a lot of jealous stares."

"What about the third? Rigel's? She has chosen?" Iason asked.

The king grimaced. "Lady Lyra of the Explorer? No, I would not wish her on anyone. Happy I am that she is Rigel's charge and not mine. Trust me when I tell you, you and Caderyn got the spoils from the good boat."

"There is a problem with the lady?" Iason blinked in surprise.

"She blames us for killing her family and refuses to listen when we tell her it was the scylla that crashed into her boat. For a while she did not speak at all and refused food. Now when she speaks it's to yell at Rigel. I sent them north, away from the palace to live in her misery."

"Poor Rigel," Iason frowned, twitching nervously as he waited for the moment he could leave the king to find his wife.

"Aye, poor indeed." The king chuckled. "I sent him with her."

"My king, I need to..." Iason glanced down the hall." In truth, he didn't know for sure where Cassandra was, only that he needed to find her. "Please."

"Aye, Lord Iason, I've kept you long enough. She is fine and at the healer's undoubtedly waiting just as anxiously for you."

Iason nodded his thanks and took off sprinting before he was properly dismissed.

Behind him, the king yelled, "I would very much like it if you could join us at the banquet. We are anxious to meet Lady Cassandra."

Iason lifted his hand but did not break stride. He could feel her now. She was close.

'*Cassandra*,' he thought, seeing the beaded doorway into the healer's home.

'*Iason?*' came her eager reply. '*Iason, where are you?*'

"Here," he said, pushing aside the beads to enter Althea's home. And then he saw her. All thoughts slipped from his mind as he looked into her green eyes. There were things he planned on saying, but instead he found himself lifting his hands to cup her face as she rushed into his arms. Her lips met his, parted and ready to accept his deep kiss. Through the haze he heard laughter, but that didn't stop him as he slid his tongue over the edge of her mouth.

'*Mm, Iason*,' she moaned through the mind link. She smelled sweet, like the sea flowers that bloomed at the water entrance of the cave. '*I can't believe you are finally here.*'

'*I ran as fast as I could. I'm sorry I wasn't in the water with you. I—*'

'*No, shh. It has all worked out. You are here now and I want to be with you. I want you...*' Her hands gripped his neck tight, holding him to her as her soft body pressed into his. '*They are watching us.*'

'*Who?*'

'*Them*,' Cassandra said, pulling back with a little giggle. She glanced over her shoulder to where

Bridget and Aidan stood, grinning like a couple of simpletons.

"Don't mind us," Bridget laughed.

'Take me somewhere,' Cassandra said only to him. *'Anywhere. I want you. I need to feel you, to know that... Please, Iason, take me somewhere we can be alone.'*

"And teach her to control her mind link," Bridget said. "We can all hear the moaning." Suddenly, she stopped and looked to the side, reaching for her temple as she nodded slowly to herself. "Ah, Caderyn's looking for me. Apparently, I have to get ready for a certain celebration banquet tonight in honor of the newest marriage." Bridget winked, and Iason knew Caderyn had been communicating privately with her from another part of the palace. "Mind links, you have to love it, unless you are trying to hide from your husband of course. When you are ready, I will teach you to block Iason out of the thoughts you don't want him to hear."

"But—" Iason began in protest, not letting his wife go. He held her tighter. A wave of protectiveness washed over him again. She was so soft. He wanted to pull the gown from her body, wanted to feel her flesh on his.

"Ah, I know what you are going to say. What

could she possibly not want you to know? But, trust me, some thoughts are private. How else are we supposed to surprise you if you always know what we're doing?"

"But—" Iason began again.

"Oh, Cassie," Bridget patted Cassandra's arm as she walked past. "I will leave you to explain that one to him."

CHAPTER 31

"Cassie?" Iason asked, not letting her go. Aidan followed Bridget from the room.

Cassandra grinned. Iason's smooth, hairless chest was bare, as were his dirty feet. Only the cloth around his waist, hanging to his knees, covered his body from view. She kept her body to his, feeling the heat through the wool tunic dress she wore. Gazing up into his face, she shivered with arousal. She loved his chiseled features, his high cheekbones and proud, strong jaw line. His green, deep set eyes pierced her. Touching his face, she ran her fingers back into his hair. "That's what they call me."

"Cassie," he said, nodding slowly as he tried the name.

"I like it when you call me Cassandra. I like the

way it sounds." Cassandra sighed, not wanting to let
him go.

"About these secrets," he began, glancing toward
the way Bridget had left. "I do not wish for there to
be any between us."

Cassandra giggled. "I think she was talking about
surprises." At his look, she added meaningfully,
"Nice surprises."

"Oh." He grinned.

"Yeah." Cassandra nodded. Moisture dampened
her sex. "Oh."

Iason glanced down between them, as if he could
sense her desire. His gaze lingered on her breasts.
Every ounce of her responded to him, and she didn't
care if he knew it. She'd never met anyone like him
before. It was as if every beat of her heart carried his
name and when she looked deep into his eyes she
knew it was the same for him.

Cassandra giggled, keeping her arms around his
strong neck. His hair stuck to his head, a result of his
run to reach her. "Didn't you say you had a home
here at the palace?"

Instead of answering, he kissed her again. His arm
swept under her legs, lifting her easily. Strong muscles
bulged against her, rippling as he moved. He carried her

into the hall, his lips still clinging to hers. Cassandra moaned, kicking her feet lightly in the air. By small degrees, he deepened the caress, letting his tongue slip over the seam of her lips. Her toes curled in anticipation, and she urged him to walk faster, to get them to privacy.

Cassandra sucked on his bottom lip before pulling back as the sound of voices caught her attention. They'd come to a tall arched entryway. Men dressed as she'd seen Iason on several occasions stood, their eyes studying them. One man wore pants like Aidan, though it didn't seem to be the most popular style. Next to them, several women chattered excitedly, glancing in her direction and giggling. A couple of the women wore long Romanesque gowns and golden coils about their heads. Others were dressed with more of an ancient Egyptian influence, complete with dark kohl lining their eyes.

Cassandra buried her head in Iason's shoulder. She felt him nod a couple times but didn't speak. After several steps had passed, he said, "We're alone now. You can look. They won't follow us."

Cassandra looked up. They were in a hallway with several doors. She moaned lightly, running her hands up into his hair, turning his head so she could kiss at his neck, picking up where she'd left off before seeing the people.

"This is the hunter's wing of the palace," Iason said. He set her down so he could open the door for her. "This is our home."

Cassandra stepped inside first, noticing how Iason stood almost nervously as he waited for approval. He shut the door behind them. Looking around, she noted it was smaller than the country estate but just as beautiful. Antique vases and urns were set on low tables. They appeared to be tarnished brass. Low, tan couches with thin blue lines woven into their cushions dominated most of the room. They looked thick and inviting.

"It's perfect." She turned to him. "This is perfect. You are perfect." Cassandra tapped a finger against his chest. "How about a bath?"

"There is a fresh water shower," he offered, motioning behind her even as he followed her beckoning gesture. "I'm sorry, but there are no bathing pools here."

"Show me," she said, liking the idea of getting him into the shower so she could bathe him.

Iason led her by the hand, taking her to a bathroom adjoining the living area. He pulled a cord hanging from the ceiling. Warm water rained from the ceiling over a wooden platform on the floor. With a tug at his waist, he pulled the material free. It dropped to the floor and he turned to her, unashamed of his nakedness. His tight ass flexed, instantly drawing her attention. His eyes lit with interest as he turned to her expectantly.

Cassandra pulled on her gown, lifting it over her head. She blushed, her lashes dipping over her eyes. A low groan sounded from her husband.

"You are lovely. I can't believe how lucky I am." Iason held his hand to her, and she took it. "I was so scared I was going to lose you."

"I was scared I had run away from the only thing that could ever make me happy," she told him. "I promise to talk to you in the future if something is wrong."

Droplets rained down over them like tiny, erotic caresses. She watched them slide over his bronzed flesh. Unable to resist, Cassandra pressed against him. She felt every curve of his body against hers, fitting perfectly. His arms tightened around her, pulling her flush to his erection. All the fear and desperation she felt melted away. This was where she belonged.

She pushed her wet hair back from her face, letting her lips glide over his flesh, kissing a path over his neck. His movements became urgent, touching her wherever he could reach, teasing her sensitive flesh.

"I love touching you," she admitted.

"And I love tasting you," he answered. Before she could blink, Iason was on his knees before her, kissing her stomach as his hands slid around to her ass. Animalistic noises escaped his throat as he glided toward her sex. *'I like kissing you to climax. I want to feel your cream on my tongue.'*

Cassandra gasped, reaching toward the narrow ledge along the shower's side to hold on. Iason inched forward, walking on his knees until he had her pressed against the wall. They were still in the full stream of the falling water.

'Open your legs to me,' he ordered. She obeyed, only to have one leg lifted up over his shoulder. *'Much better.'*

He moaned into her, his lips excitedly closing over her sex. His tongue drew along her folds, licking the shower water mixed with her cream. Cassandra made a loud noise of approval before catching herself. She bit her lip, not sure how thin the walls were between the hunter's homes.

'Scream all you want,' Iason said, as if reading her concern.

She gave a nervous laugh. "I will have to get used to you being in there."

Even so, there was something freeing about being unable to hide any part of herself, and knowing Iason accepted her—faults and all. His mouth continued to work its magic, his head bumping along her thigh. He grabbed her legs, gripping them tight.

'Ecstasy. Perfection.' His thoughts were hers, blending as the pleasure built inside her.

She arched into his mouth, the water against her breasts making her nipples tingle with sensation. He thrust his tongue into her passage, working it in and out in an almost supernatural rhythm. Then, suddenly, he latched his mouth around her clit, creating a seal as his tongue swirled the sensitive bud. She tensed, giving small cries of approval. 'Yes, yes, oh, yes!'

Groaning loudly, she came, bucking against him. Iason didn't stop as his hands replaced his mouth. He stood before her, stroking her sex. She felt insatiable.

"Honestly, I've been able to think of little else since I awoke at the healers. Why is that?" Cassandra wiggled, feeling insatiable.

"We call it the affliction. It happens after we've been shifted for longer periods of time. Sexual release helps to even out our energies after shifting."

"Well," she paused, reaching between his thighs, "I see you have an affliction."

"Aye." He rocked his hips into her.

"Come inside me," she begged. "I want you in me. Now."

Iason lifted her off the platform, holding her legs to the side so he could enter her. The tip of his erection, so firm and ready, brushed against her slit. She angled her body, holding onto his shoulders for support. He thrust in, giving her all of him with one heavy thrust. She moaned at the deep penetration, her body instantly adjusting to his size.

He held her hips, thrusting deeply at a slow pace. She closed her eyes, savoring each sensation. Her fingers slipped on his wet flesh, gliding over the bulging biceps. His grunts of pleasure surrounded her. She clamped the muscles of her passage, squeezing him hard. His rhythm faltered.

"I love the feel of you on me," he managed between panting breaths. "Squeeze me again."

She did and he began slamming his hips harder, riding her almost violently. Cassandra didn't mind, this was exactly what she wanted. His thoughts mingled inside her, mixing with her own, until they were nothing more than a series of grunts and moans of shared passion. There were no secrets between them. She felt what he felt, heard what he thought. The tension built, until suddenly, her body shook with climax.

Iason's cry joined her's and she knew he was coming, even as he continued to pump into her. Then, with a groan, he froze, his tight body trembling with complete and utter release.

Iason let her body slip down so her legs were once more on the floor. Her back stung from where it had rubbed along the shower wall, but she didn't care. Cupping her face, he whispered, "You are amazing."

Cassandra blushed.

"Even now there is some innocence in you," he chuckled.

Reaching to the side, he took the shampoo and rubbed it into his hair, washing it as she did the same. Conditioner followed and the sweet smell of herbs wafted around them. Then, grabbing soap, Iason began to lather his body. Cassandra watched with interest, only to do the same when he offered her the soap to clean herself up with. She washed her body, her eyes staying on him, following his hands. The suds felt great against her flesh and she became aroused by the look of Iason's hands on his body. Her breath caught as he fisted his rising cock, cleaning it with slow, twisting movements. Before she realized it, she was touching herself, too.

His rhythm picked up, as he pumped his fist harder and faster. Cassandra moaned, reaching a tiny orgasm. Their rapid breath mingled. The shower washed the soap from them almost too quickly.

Iason reached for the cord, pulling it so the shower turned off. Cassandra shivered at the cool change in temperature. He handed her a large wool towel to dry off with, only to take it from her when she tried to wrap her naked body with it.

Dropping the towel on the floor, Iason pulled her to him once more. He kissed her, his lips desperately moving as if he would swallow her whole. The hard press of his damp flesh rippled along her body as he walked her backward toward the living area. She expected him to take her to a bedroom and was surprised when he stopped instead by the low couch.

Laying her down gently, he continued to kiss her, working his way over her body in worshipping caresses. His tongue drew along her neck, danced over her collarbone, swirled her breasts and licked a fiery trail down her stomach. He kneeled on the floor, pulling her hips so her legs hung over the edge of the bench-like seat. There was no arm to block him as he nibbled her inner thigh.

'*Ah!*' She jumped at the tender bite and he instantly kissed it better. His mouth worked to her center fire, beginning anew the agonizing pleasure of his intimate kisses. Even her bones felt like they'd turned to liquid.

'*So delicate,*' he told her, almost as if the thought slipped unawares from his mind. '*So fragile and sweet.*'

As much as she enjoyed his passionate kisses, she wanted to feel him against her even more. Pulling on his arm, she urged him up. Her hips squirmed and her legs parted.

'*Please,*' she thought, too breathless with passion to speak the words. '*I want you inside me. Do not make me wait, Iason. I want you now.*'

Iason moaned at her words, his expression saying he needed her just as badly. She pulled harder and he brought his body to hers, still kneeling at the end of the couch. His body pushed up slightly, as if he had moved a foot on the floor, half crouching, half kneeling. She arched into him as his shaft rubbed along her slit. It felt so good. Her body was wet for him and he slid easily inside her.

She ran her hands over his chest, pulling him toward her. He pushed her up on the couch with his hips, keeping their bodies joined. Her leg fell over the side to make room. It wasn't the best position, but the urgency of the moment outweighed any discomfort.

His wet hair tickled her fingers as she touched his face and neck. Her foot dug into the floor, using it as leverage when he began to move. She loved watching his strong body, flexing and moving, the muscles rippling beneath tanned flesh. He fitted himself deep, only to pull out.

Iason controlled his hips, thrusting with perfect tempo. He stayed deep, working in fast, vibrating circles. The centuries in water clearly had strengthened him to the point of perfection. Cassandra dug her hands into his shoulders, the nails biting his flesh slightly. She felt his pleasure as if it were her own.

"Feels good," she managed, gasping. *'So good. Don't stop. Never stop.'*

She held on tight as a first, hard climax hit her. Her body weakened, but he kept pushing, slowing, only to build her right back up. The vibrating circles intensified. Cassandra jerked hard, panting loudly now. She came again, just as hard as the first time only now her body was so sensitive that every little jolt seemed like it set her on fire. He continued to thrust, fast and deep. She came a third time, her body tensing so she couldn't even move. Iason's cry of victory echoed in her mind and he climaxed, releasing his seed inside of her.

Breathing hard, his body weakened, falling forward as he braced his weight on his arm. Damp hair brushed her cheek as he moved. She moaned softly, unable to say a word. Not rolling off, he kept the bulk of his weight off her, trapping her beneath him. He pulled out, nuzzling her neck with kisses, moaning in soft contentment. His mouth brushed the corner of her parted lips.

After some time had passed and their breathing slowed, Iason pulled away. She didn't move, enjoying watching him as he stood next to her.

'I can't believe how incredibly handsome you are,' she thought.

His smile widened and his deep green eyes seemed to sparkle.

Cassandra frowned, horrified as she sat up. "Oh, no!"

"What?" he asked, instantly kneeling in concern. "What is it? What has happened?"

"Can they hear me?" she whispered, her eyes wide and tearful. "The others in the palace, can they hear my thoughts? Because I thought that thing about your... And, um, your..." She made a weak noise even as he chuckled. "It's not funny. They are all going to think I'm..."

"What? Beautiful? Loved? Cherished? Sexy? Married to an incredibly lucky husband?"

"Wanton!" Cassandra cried.

"They didn't hear you," he laughed. *'And I don't care that you are wanton. I like wanton.'*

"Oh," she instantly relaxed. "You are sure? Because Bridget was saying something about a banquet tonight and if I have to go anywhere I wouldn't be able to face the palace, let alone a king, if they'd heard me."

"You were concentrating on me, so the thoughts went only to me." Iason kissed the tip of her nose before pulling her up to stand with him. He led her to a door next to the bathroom. It was his bedroom, as simply decorated as the rest of the house. Though living in the palace would be nice, she found she missed the country estate.

"We will go back there," he said in answer to the thought. "But I hope you can find pleasure here in the palace as well. I am sure Aidan and Bridget will help you find your way around and you are welcome to decorate or do whatever you wish to this home." Cassandra crawled on the bed, lying down on the covers. He was instantly next to her, settling his body along hers. He kissed her temple lightly, wrapping her in his arms. "Can you be happy here, at the palace? It is where I would like you to stay when I am away on a hunt."

"I can be happy anywhere, as long as I'm with you," she said. "But, about these hunts."

"Aye?"

"You will be careful, right?" She looked deep into his eyes, letting him feel her worry and her acceptance. "I know what you do is important, even if the humans you save don't realize it. I will never ask you to stop hunting, but promise me you will be careful when you do and will come home to me."

"I promise. I have a reason to live. I have you." He again kissed her temple lightly.

"What do you do with the scylla once you catch them?" Cassandra snuggled into his warmth and closed her eyes. "They won't escape to hurt others will they?"

"They are imprisoned and many of them die within a few short days once they are out of the ocean." He sighed. "They are not treated cruelly, but to let them free is to sentence many to death."

She nodded, understanding. Her body was content and nothing else in the world or ocean mattered. "You are a good man, Iason, and you make me very proud to be your wife. I love you."

"I love you, too, my sweet Cassandra." His grip on her side tightened as he hugged her to him.

Suddenly, a knock sounded on the outside door. Iason chuckled, but didn't answer.

"What is it?" she asked.

"Probably someone coming to fetch us for the banquet we are missing," he answered.

"That's now?"

"Aye."

Cassandra didn't want to get up and, by her husband's lack of movement, he didn't want to either.

"What's it for?" she asked.

"So that the king may announce our marriage. The celebration is for us."

"We are married, though, right?" She asked, struggling to sit up. He held her tighter.

"Aye, we are. Let them celebrate without us. I have all the feasting I want right here." He glanced down her body meaningfully. She giggled, lightly swatting his arm.

"Won't we get into trouble?" Cassandra closed her eyes.

"Aye, but I will just have you give one of your

sweet smiles to the king and all will be forgiven. With your pretty face, who could stay mad?"

The knock sounded louder than before. They both laughed, not moving to answer.

'*I love you,*' she thought, letting a peaceful sleep claim her.

'*And I you, my wife, and I you.*'

The End

THE SERIES CONTINUES...

The Mighty Hunter
Commanding the Tides
Captive of the Deep
Surrender to the Sea
Making Waves
The Merman King

Captive of the Deep
Lords of the Abyss Book 3

Rigel has searched for an end to his people's curse. Living in the lost city of Atlantes, women are rare and immortality has come with a high price--loneliness. When a beautiful female is thrown into the ocean, her fate is in his hands, and this sexy mortal is more than this hard up warrior can resist.

Chapter One Excerpt

Lyra Harne hated the ocean. She hated the smell of fish, the taste of salt on her tongue, the briny smell in the air when the waves crashed against the wooden ship. She hated the creaking of the hull and the endless rocking, back and forth, back and forth, back and forth. Holding her hand over her mouth, she tried not to gag. It was a complete exercise in uselessness. Her stomach hit the railing as she puked over the side.

The fast clip of the wooden ship against the waves sent high splashes of water over the sides. Lyra was drenched, but she didn't dare move as she held tightly to the rail. Her heart pounded and for a moment it was only her, the rail and the long stretch of moonlit ocean, and the endless rocking back and forth, back and forth, back and...

"Just kill me now," she moaned to no one in particular, as she twisted the cap on her mouthwash.

The taste of mint had become as familiar as the smell of salt, and just as hated. The few people milling around the deck were used to seeing her bent over in misery. She'd been that way for the last two months as they sailed from Spain to the Americas. The only reason she was on this ship was because her brothers and father needed her help. A very rich man paid big money for her family's sailing expertise. Her father, Captain Bill Harne, was the best of the best. It was said he could sail through a hurricane and come out smiling. Her oldest brother, Will, had been born for the ocean and probably spent more of his life on sea than land. The others—Jackson, Kristopher, Rocky and Winston—had varying levels of experience, but all of them were strong swimmers and dedicated to lives on the sea. Then there was Lyra, the baby of the family, spoiled by her mother and kept on land while her brothers braved the corners of the Earth. Her mom had been desperate to have something other than a sailor in the family. She'd ended up with Lyra, who wasn't really much of anything.

"Mom would have laughed to see you now," Jackson teased. "She would've said it served you right for agreeing to this trip."

"The seasickness or this hideous dress?" She glanced down at what could only be described as bar wench gone to sea. At least her brothers looked like respectable men from the 1500s. It was all part of the deal with the rich boss. He wanted the authentic Spanish Armanda experience. Apparently, the guy's great-great-great-something-or-other was an important part of Spain's history. The truth was, whenever the man spoke about it, Lyra's mind fuzzed out and she stopped paying attention.

"Now that you mention it, that gown does look a little less bulky." Jackson glanced at the skirt.

"I threw the petticoats overboard." Lyra grinned through her physical discomfort. "You try wearing a corset and fifty pounds worth of material on a rocking death trap. I still say that I should be able to dress like a lad. I'd give anything for a linen shirt and breeches at this point."

"Not up to me," Jackson said, slapping the pads on his arms. He wore an old fashioned linen ruff around his neck, an embroidered, padded epaulet, short stockings and puffed shorts much like those worn on the old Armada galleons. "This isn't how I would have spent my fortune." He eyed her with mock curiosity. "How is it you swam in from the same gene pool as the rest of us?"

"I'm pretty sure the family gene pool was dried

up and I just kind of crawled in." She gave a wry laugh.

"You know, you could have said no to the trip."

"You all begged me to come. I'm the only one out of you sorry lot that can speak Spanish." She gave him a sheepish look, not feeling better, but definitely glad to have an empty stomach.

"I suppose it's better for you here than hanging by yourself at home. Mom wouldn't have wanted you to become a shut-in either."

"I'm not a shut-in. My job is online. I stay home and work." It had been three years since her mother's death and Lyra still missed her. Not wanting to talk about it, she said, "Tell me a story. Distract me."

"Did I ever tell you about the time we docked in Antwerp?" Jackson grinned. His devilish looks had been the ruination of many a young heart, but his heart had never been stolen. Hair as black as midnight and eyes that twinkled like stars—that was Jackson. And Kris. And Will. And Rocky. And Winston. Heck, even their father. Lyra took after her mom with dark blonde hair down to her waist and wide green eyes. Right now her hair was bound back at her nape to keep it out of her face.

"Yes," Lyra answered, "you did."

"East London Harbor in South Africa?"

"Yes."

"Robben Island on the Western Cape?"

"Yes."

"Hong Kong? Rotterdam? Pohang?"

"Yes, yes, and, oh please, not that one again yes." Lyra laughed, covering her ears, as her brother successfully distracted her from her seasickness. "Don't you have stories that aren't all about you and some lady you met at port?"

"Sure, but those aren't the good ones." Jackson motioned that she should follow him. "You empty? We should go. Captain needs you to translate."

"Man, I hope I don't have anything left," she muttered grabbing her stomach. "How long until this is over?"

"Less than a month," Jackson answered. "And about two hours less than the last time you ask—"

He never finished the sentence. The boat pitched to the side with a loud crack. Lyra screamed as her arms flailed in the air. She could see Jackson's expression fill with panic and concern as he reached for her. His hand missed her arm and she flew into the railing with a bruising thud. Her ribs throbbed in agony. Automatically, she grabbed at the first thing she could find, a long wooden post beneath the rail, and held on for dear life as the boat pitched in the other direction. Her legs tangled in the skirts as she slid over the deck.

The next seconds were the most horrific in her life. Men emerged from below deck only to be swept away as the ship was jarred again and again. She couldn't help them even though she tried to stop a few as they slipped past her legs, but could barely hold on herself. Jackson was swept away trying to reach her, captured by a rush of water over the deck. Lyra screamed again and again, begging and pleading, demanding that whatever it was stopped. But, in the end, it was no use.

"Monsters," a man yelled in broken English. "They come from below!"

To find out more about Michelle's books visit www.MichellePillow.com

ABOUT MICHELLE M. PILLOW

New York Times & *USA TODAY*
Bestselling Author

Michelle loves to travel and try new things, whether it's a paranormal investigation of an old Vaudeville Theatre or climbing Mayan temples in Belize. She believes life is an adventure fueled by copious amounts of coffee.

Newly relocated to the American South, Michelle is involved in various film and documentary projects with her talented director husband. She is mom to a fantastic artist. And she's managed by a dog and cat who make sure she's meeting her deadlines.

For the most part she can be found wearing pajama pants and working in her office. There may or may not be dancing. It's all part of the creative process.

**Come say hello! Michelle loves talking
with readers on social media!**

www.MichellePillow.com

facebook.com/AuthorMichellePillow

twitter.com/michellepillow

instagram.com/michellempillow

bookbub.com/authors/michelle-m-pillow

goodreads.com/Michelle_Pillow

amazon.com/author/michellepillow

youtube.com/michellepillow

pinterest.com/michellepillow

COMPLIMENTARY EXCERPTS

LOVE POTIONS EXERPT

BY MICHELLE M. PILLOW

Warlocks MacGregor® **Book 1**

Contemporary Paranormal Scottish Warlocks

A little magickal mischief never hurt anyone...

Erik MacGregor, from a clan of ancient Scottish warlocks, isn't looking for love. After centuries, it's not even a consideration...until he moves in next door to Lydia Barratt. It's clear that the shy beauty wants nothing to do with him, but he's drawn to her nonetheless and determined to win her over.

Lydia Barratt just wants to be left alone to grow flowers and make lotions in her old Victorian house. The last thing she needs is a demanding Scottish man meddling in her private life. Just because he's gorgeous and totally rocks a kilt doesn't mean she's going to fall for his seductive manner.

But Erik won't give up and just as Lydia let's her guard down, his sister decides to get involved. Her little love potion prank goes terribly wrong, making Lydia the target of his sudden embarrassingly obsessive behavior. They'll have to find a way to pull Erik out of the spell fast when it becomes clear that Lydia has more than a lovesick warlock to worry about. Evil lurks within the shadows and it plans to use Lydia, alive or dead, to take out Erik and his clan for good.

Love Potions Excerpt

"Ly-di-ah! I sit beneath your window, laaaass, singing 'cause I loooove your a—"

"For the love of St. Francis of Assisi, someone call a vet. There is an injured animal screaming in pain outside," Charlotte interrupted the flow of music in ill-humor.

Lydia lifted her forehead from the kitchen table. Her windows and doors were all locked, and yet Erik's endlessly verbose singing penetrated the barrier of glass and wood with ease.

Charlotte held her head and blinked heavily. Her red-rimmed eyes were filled with the all too poignant look of a hangover. She took a seat at the table and laid her head down. Her moan sounded something like, "I'm never moving again."

"You need fluids," Lydia prescribed, getting up to pour unsweetened herbal tea from the pitcher in the fridge. She'd mixed it especially for her friend. It was Gramma Annabelle's hangover recipe of willow bark, peppermint, carrot, and ginger. The old lady always had a fresh supply of it in the house while she was alive. Apparently, being a natural witch also meant in partaking in natural liquors. Annabelle had kept a steady supply of moonshine stashed in the basement. If the concert didn't stop soon she might try to find an old bottle.

"*Ly-di-ah!*"

"Omigod. Kill me," Charlotte moaned. "No. Kill him. Then kill me."

"*Ly-di-ah!*"

Erik had been singing for over an hour. At first, he'd tried to come inside. She'd not invited him and the barrier spell sent him sprawling back into the yard. He didn't seem to mind as he found a seat on some landscaping timbers and began his serenade. The last time she'd asked him to be quiet, he'd gotten louder and overly enthusiastic. In fact, she'd been too scared to pull back the curtains for a clearer look, but she was pretty sure he'd been dancing on her lawn, shaking his kilt.

"Omigod," Charlotte muttered, pushing up and angrily going to a window. Then grimacing, she said, "Is he wearing a tux jacket with his kilt?"

"Don't let him see you," Lydia cried out in a panic. It was too late. The song began with renewed force.

"He's..." Charlotte frowned. "I think it's dancing."

Since the damage was done, Lydia joined Charlotte at the window. Erik grinned. He lifted his arms to the side and kicked his legs, bouncing around the yard like a kid on too much sugar. "Maybe it's a traditional Scottish dance?"

Both women tilted their heads in unison as his kilt kicked up to show his perfectly formed ass.

"He's not wearing..." Charlotte began.

"I know. He doesn't," Lydia answered. Damn, the man had a fine body. Too bad Malina's trick had turned him insane.

To find out more about Michelle's books visit www.MichellePillow.com

PLEASE LEAVE A REVIEW

THANK YOU FOR READING!

Please take a moment to share your thoughts by reviewing this book.

Be sure to check out Michelle's other titles at www.MichellePillow.com